ROYALLY ELECTED

HER ROYAL HAREM, BOOK THREE

CATHERINE BANKS

TURBO KITTEN

Turbo Kitten Industries™

P.O. Box 5012

Galt, CA 95632

www.turbokitten.us

Catherine Banks

www.catherinebanks.com

www.turbokitten.us/catherine-banks

CHAPTER 1

"**F**ly or die!" Emrys roared.

Three of my four guards lay unconscious on the ground, blood pooled beneath them. They were alive, but barely.

Nico panted heavily, cuts all over his body, and his magic fizzling. Soon, he would fall too.

Emrys and Nico battled the army of vampires and dhampir before us, but there were too many.

"I can't," I cried, my hands shaking and my knees weak. My fear of dying at the hands of the enemy was equal to that of flying in my dragon form.

"If you don't, they'll all die!" Emrys, King of the Dragons, yelled at me. His black hair waved in the wind and specks of blood marred its beauty.

Dozens of dead dhampirs littered the field, and piles of ashes from dead vampires crushed underfoot. Among them were also the bodies of my friends, some dead, and some gravely wounded. On one side of the field Dan, King and Alpha of the Werewolves, battled against six dhampirs while Johann, King of the Mages, battled six more behind him.

Chaos. Death and destruction surrounded me.

"Fly!" Emrys roared, his eyes flashing emerald before he shifted, he jumped into the fray, distracting the enemies to give me a chance to flee.

A dhampir stabbed Nico in the stomach and Nico coughed up blood.

"No!" I screamed, tears streaming down my face.

"Jolie!" Rhys yelled.

I sat upright and blinked the dream away. My cheeks were wet with tears and my hands shook.

Rhys pulled me into a hug and stroked my hair. "I'm here," he whispered. "I'm safe and unhurt."

More arms wrapped around me from behind.

"It was just a dream," Fox whispered and I felt his magic wrap around me, a cocoon of warmth and happiness. It couldn't penetrate the fear and distress I felt.

"I need out," I whispered in a strangled voice.

They immediately released me and slid across the bed to give me space. My feet hit the floor and I wrapped my arms around myself.

Deryn walked into the room in his boxers. He looked amazing, but I wasn't in the mood to admire all the muscles on display. He tried to embrace me, but I dodged his hands and rushed to the bathroom.

I turned the shower on and sat on the floor of the tub, letting the warm water hit me.

For the past two weeks, I'd been having the same dream. Every time I woke up in tears. The guys tried to assure me it was just a dream, just my mind's way of processing all the drama that had unfolded since meeting the Four Princes of Jinla.

I wasn't so sure. I couldn't fly yet, despite my many lessons with Emrys. Flying scared me. What if I shifted mid-flight? My shifts were unpredictable at times. Plus, the dream just felt too real. I worried it was a premonition.

"Jolie," Nico called.

"No," I replied, knowing he would want to come in.

"You closed our bonds," he said. "Please, release them."

Unconsciously, my mind shut down the bonds between me and my four guards when I experienced extreme emotional situations. They hated when I did it because it reminded them of the time our bonds had been severed by Justina.

I exhaled and released the clamps from each of their bonds. Their worry, pain, and love rushed to me. I gasped and struggled to ground myself for several moments. No matter how many times it happened, I was never prepared for the onslaught of their emotions.

"Thank you," Nico called through the door, then he walked away.

After washing and brushing my teeth, I returned to my room. When I had first moved in, I had a queen-sized bed and a dresser. Now, a custom double king bed took up half of the room and my three-drawer dresser had been replaced by a huge dresser with nine drawers.

Rhys sat alone on my bed, his hair much longer than when I had met him. The side swept bangs reached just below his left eyebrow. He wore a pair of jeans and a black t-shirt that hugged his chest. My eyes caught on the crystal imbedded in his cheek, but I looked at his chest instead.

"Are you going to tell us the full dream yet?" he asked, a scowl pulling his eyebrows together.

I wasn't ready to tell them that the four of them were defeated in the dream. They all assumed something had happened by the way I cried and clung to them the first few times.

Turning, I dug through the dresser for clothes without replying.

He sighed and left the room, a cloud of worry and anger surrounded him and flowed down our bond. He quickly shut down the bond, which made me stumble and slide to my knees on the carpet.

That did hurt!

It took me a moment to compose myself, stand and find my

clothes. Once I finished getting dressed and ready, I walked out of my apartment, down the stairs, and out to the waiting black SUV. Overhead, the bright blue sky felt too cheerful for my dark mood.

Deryn and Martin stopped talking when I climbed into the front passenger seat and Deryn looked out his window in the back, giving me the cold shoulder.

I checked our bond and it was open. So, why was he mad?

"Hello, beautiful," Martin said before putting the car in drive.

"Morning," I replied and looked out my own window.

The drive to the pack was tense and silent. I jumped out before Martin put the SUV in park and marched to the house. Deryn didn't follow.

Dan opened the door before I made it to the house. He smiled wide and said, "There's my girl!" He took two steps to close the distance and pulled me into a tight hug.

He made me feel loved and safe, just like an alpha should.

"Hi, Dan," I whispered.

He pushed me out to arm's length and scowled. "What's wrong?" Without waiting for me to answer, he looked behind me. "Where's my son?"

I shrugged. "In the car still, probably."

"Are you two fighting?" he asked.

I sighed. "I don't know. He's giving me the silent treatment and I didn't do anything. Well, that I can think of."

"Did you seal your mating bond yet?" Dan asked softly.

"No," I admitted. "But, we just haven't had time. I've been working a lot and he's been at a lot of meetings with you."

"Have you sealed it with any of them?"

I blushed and looked at my feet. "No."

"Are you having second thoughts?"

"No!" I snapped and looked up to meet his eyes. "Not at all." Not that I could anyway. We were technically mates now, but each clan had different ways of sealing the bond. I hadn't sealed the bond with any of them to fully become their mate.

"Do they know that?" Dan asked, a knowing look in his eyes.

"I, uh…they should," I said and sighed, looking back down. "I guess I haven't really been talking much to them lately."

"Want to talk about it?"

"It's a dream I keep having."

"The same one?"

"Same exact one."

"And they die?"

I met his eyes again. "What?"

He smirked. "He told me you were having a recurring dream and you weren't telling them the full story."

"What if it's a premonition?" I asked and gulped.

"It could be."

I groaned. "Dan, that's *not* reassuring."

He draped his arms around my shoulders and steered me towards the gymnasium. "You need to tell your mates what you see. They need to know so that they can prepare for it. Just in case it is a premonition."

I hated talking about it. My anxiety spiked, and I always cried.

"Fine," I whispered, resigned to do as he said. If it was a premonition, they could prepare better by knowing what happened in the dream.

He pushed open the door, and the sounds of the basketball game inside blasted out to greet us. Many pack members sat in the stands, watching the other pack members playing basketball. Dan led me to the stands, pulling me down to the bench beside him. A few teenagers scooted closer to Dan, talking to him about their schooling.

He was so loved by his pack, it made me smile to see him interacting with the younger werewolves.

Martin and Deryn joined the game and began to play basketball with their pack mates. They moved fast across the court.

Human sports didn't entertain me, but when Others played them, it became something else. Something super intense.

"Auntie!" Martin's twin daughters, Tamara & Madison, yelled and rushed up the stands to hug me.

I hugged them back and kissed their heads. "Hello, nieces."

Sharla came and over and sat next to me, picking up Madison to take her spot. "Hey," she said in greeting.

I hugged her with one arm. "Hey."

"When did you get here?" Sharla asked.

"Just a couple of minutes ago," I answered.

A bell sounded, ending the quarter. The guys went to the tables on the sidelines and drank water from the cooler there. Deryn glanced in my direction, then looked away.

I sighed loud and dropped my head.

"What's wrong?" Sharla asked.

"Nothing I want to talk about," I told her and leaned my shoulder against hers.

"I'm here if you want to talk," she whispered.

I nodded but said nothing. I wouldn't spread my relationship issues around.

"I thought I smelled something delicious," a deep male voice said.

Sharla moved to sit in front of me, pulling the girls down with her, giving the newcomer the place at my side.

I leapt up and threw my arms around Thor, the giant were-wolf picked me up as he hugged me. "Thor!" I screeched.

He squeezed me and kissed my cheek. "Jo, I've missed you."

He set me on my feet but kept his hands on my waist. "I've missed you too," I told him with a wide smile. "What are you doing here?"

"I'm here on a mission for a couple months," Thor explained.

"And I'm just now finding out?" I asked with a frown.

He chuckled and pulled me into another hug. "I just got here, Jo. I hadn't had time to tell you."

"You could have texted me," I reminded him.

"Thor," Deryn called.

Thor turned, draping his arm around my shoulders. "Yeah?"

"Why don't you come play with us?" Deryn asked, his eyes glued to the hand on my shoulder.

"No, thanks," Thor said and sat, pulling me against his side as he did.

Deryn's eyes shifted and his fists clenched.

"So, you gave him a mating crystal, but haven't sealed it yet?" Thor asked in a whisper in my ear. "Why not?"

I blushed and turned away. "None of your business."

"Thor," Deryn growled. "Stop pushing me."

Thor sighed and pulled his arm away. "You're no fun."

I stood, grabbed Thor's hand, and led him down the stands. "Come on, I need to talk to you."

Deryn growled but didn't follow.

I let the door slam shut behind us, then exhaled and leaned my forehead against Thor's arm. "Damn him," I whispered.

"What's up, Jo? Why is he acting crazy again?" Thor asked.

"I'm not one hundred percent sure, but it's probably a couple things lumped together," I said softly.

"Did you really need to talk to me?" he asked.

I shook my head and started walking towards the back of the pack's territory. "No. I just needed to get out of there. Sorry for dragging you with me."

"Don't apologize. If you need me, I'm here. For *anything*," he said and waggled his eyebrows.

I laughed and punched his arm. "Knock it off."

He laughed and draped his arm around my shoulders again. "So, what's new? What's happened since I last saw you two months ago?"

Two months? Had it really been that long?

"Not much. I've been really busy with work and the guys have been really busy with their clans."

"So, not much alone time?" he asked.

"No," I admitted. "It's partially their fault. Ever since that night, they haven't wanted to be apart for more than a few hours."

"Jo, they lost you. They lost their bond with you, felt it sever. You almost died afterwards and there was nothing they could do about it. It's not something you can just get over."

I knew that.

"It wasn't a picnic for me either," I muttered.

He squeezed my shoulders. "Just give them a break. And mate with them!"

I cringed. "I know."

Thor hugged me and rubbed my back. "It'll be okay, Jo. I'm here, so you can call on me if you need me."

I returned his hug, then pulled back, feeling Deryn's anger. "He's behind me, isn't he?"

Thor smirked. "A hundred yards and closing."

"I'll text you later, okay?" I asked.

He nodded, kissed my cheek, then walked off.

Deryn's anger decreased as he stopped by me. "What did you two talk about?" he asked.

I turned and arched an eyebrow. "Now you're talking to me?"

He stepped forward and rested his head on top of mine but said nothing.

"If my dreams are premonitions, I don't know what to do. If it comes to pass…" I couldn't finish that sentence.

He slid his hands up my arms and whispered, "Baby, you've had nightmares since we met you. Why are these different?"

"They just feel different. They feel real. They don't feel like normal nightmares."

"When we get home, will you please tell us the full dream?"

I gripped his shirt and pulled myself closer to him. "Yes."

He wrapped me up and held me in silence for several minutes. "I love you, baby. I don't like it when you're upset and hold shit in instead of talking to us."

"Can you please release our bond fully?" I asked softly.

"What?" he asked, then I felt it open and sagged into him. "Sorry, I hadn't realized that I had done that."

I nodded and stepped back, rubbing my heart. There was still one bond not open.

"Who else?" Deryn asked and placed his warm hand on my sternum.

"Rhys," I whispered. "He's mad at me."

"Let's head back. It's lunch time," he said, changing the subject rather quickly.

We locked fingers and walked to the house. Being able to touch them in public was nice. It took the edge off the pain when one was closed off to me.

"I'll be right in. Save me a seat," Deryn said, letting go of my hand.

I kissed his cheek and walked inside, shutting the door, but stayed by it to eavesdrop.

"Hey, asshole," Deryn said on the phone to whoever he called. "You're hurting her." There was a pause then he growled, "You closed your bond, idiot."

Rhys released the bond and I felt his worry and apology. I staggered forward and caught myself against the wall while my knees wobbled. His emotions were always so much stronger than the others.

Deryn walked in and rushed to my side. "Jolie?" he asked.

"I'm fine," I whispered. "Rhys opened our bond and it caught me off guard."

He helped me up and wiped a tear away from my cheek with his thumb. "We're all still getting used to the bonds. They aren't the same as our warrior bonds."

"I know," I whispered. "Then we'll be adding our full mating bonds on top of that."

"So, you still plan to mate with us?" he asked.

I reached up and touched the crystal embedded under his eye.

"Yes. We've all been busy and haven't had alone time with the right circumstances to seal them."

He nodded. "I know. It's still nice to hear it."

"I'm sorry. I should have made it a priority—"

He silenced me with a kiss and smiled. "It's alright. We know we will be your mates eventually."

I touched the stone again. "Yeah, but people already think—"

"Good," he said adamantly. "Soon we will get yours finished."

"Don't I have to have one for each of you?"

"We don't think so. Nico has been working on getting all our blood and connections into one. He's been having trouble, but we know it's possible."

"I wouldn't mind having four," I said softly.

"Good to know," he replied.

"Lunch!" Dan boomed.

"Food!" Tamara and Madison yelled, raced down the stairs, and past us to the dining room. They didn't live in the house anymore, but they might as well have with how often they were here.

We followed them and took seats at the dining table alongside Dan, Thor, Martin, Sharla, and the girls. Dan chatted with Martin and Sharla while Deryn chatted with Thor. It was a nice home cooked meal and I loved being a part of it.

Looking at the girls, I could imagine Deryn helping his own children cut up their meat or making silly faces at them…like he was doing now. He would make a great father.

But, not with me.

Sorrow filled me, tightening my chest painfully.

"Excuse me," I whispered, set my napkin down, and raced to the bathroom. I gripped the counter and bit my lip to stop the sobs trying to escape.

I deprived them of so much by being their mate. I wasn't worth it. My love wasn't worth it.

Deryn tried to open the door and sighed softly when he found it locked. "Baby, what's wrong?"

I flushed the toilet, opened the bathroom window, and leapt out. Thankfully, I landed in a crouch and the impact only hurt my legs a little.

Thor looked at me from the dining room window, his eyes widened, and he stood up, his mouth opening, likely calling Deryn.

I shifted into my dragon form and jumped up a bit so I was floating above the ground—not really flying, but not touching the ground. I banked left, towards the back half of the forest. I landed in a rolling heap, but somehow avoided injuring my wings. I hated flying as a dragon. It was scary, but I was trying to overcome it with small flights.

Deryn tugged on our bond and I gently placed a shield around it, to prevent him from finding me. I did the same to the others' bonds as well.

What was I going to do? They claimed they didn't care, but part of them did. Part of them wanted heirs.

I didn't want to have four children. Childbirth was painful. Plus, there was always the possibility of having two of Deryn's kids and none of Fox's, or something like that. Nature wasn't fair.

Curling up beneath a massive oak tree, I let out the pain. I sobbed and howled my pain. The pain of knowing I wasn't worthy. The pain of knowing a small piece of them would always resent me. The pain of knowing I cost the men I loved so much.

Nico, Rhys, Fox, and Deryn popped into existence a few feet away from me. All four looked at me while clutching their chests.

"Go," I whispered.

All four dropped to their knees and groaned.

"What's wrong?" Fox asked and started to shuffle towards me. "How did you find me?"

"We can always locate you now," Nico said.

"I'm not worth this…all this pain," I whispered.

11

"Stop bottling it up and talk to us, please," Rhys begged.

"Love is stupid!" I snapped. "It makes you do stupid things."

All four cringed.

"You chose me, but why? I don't want kids, but you all do. You all would make great fathers. What if I have two kids from one of you and none for the others? Your lives are run by schedules now. We don't come home and spontaneously jump into bed, not when there's three more of you also being affected by my scent. We haven't had time to even mate, yet all four of you have my crystal.

"Mating may not be the best idea. If my dreams are right, you're all going to die protecting me. You're all going to die because I am a burden. I don't add any substance to your lives. I'm not politically savvy. I'm not magically gifted. I have quirks like being able to tell dragons apart, but nothing useful. I make crap compared to you four. I don't contribute. I'm a hinderance."

"Well, now that you got all of that off your chest, how do you feel?" a squeaky male voice asked.

"Is that—" Rhys began.

"No way," Deryn whispered.

"They're real?" Nico asked.

I turned and looked behind me. A tall red fox with nine tails grinned at me, his tails fanned out behind him proudly.

"A kistune?" I asked and wiped at my face.

He bowed. "I'm Nar, a relative of Foxfire's."

"I didn't summon him," Fox said loudly.

Nar sat in front of me. "He's been complaining about not being able to help you. I thought I could assist."

I almost said thank you out of politeness, but I wasn't thankful. I hadn't wanted to say all of that to them.

"You're trespassing," Deryn told Nar, but he looked more intrigued than mad.

"Technically you brought me here," Nar said. "I've been

working on her for a week." Nar looked at me. "You're very strong-willed."

"Thank you?" I wasn't certain if it was a compliment or not.

"Can we have some privacy?" Fox asked Nar.

Nar looked at me and whispered, "Summon me if you're in danger."

"How?" I asked as he started to become see through.

He dropped a piece of paper with a kitsune drawn on it. "Put it on your skin and it'll add a tattoo. Then you'll just need to tap me, uh the tattoo, and I'll help."

He disappeared and I stared at the piece of paper on the ground.

"Jolie," Fox whispered.

I looked up at the four men staring at me. "What?" I whispered.

"We need to talk about this," Rhys said.

"I know," I admitted. I picked up the paper and walked to them.

Nico grabbed my hand, then the rest set their hands on him and Nico teleported us to the apartment. We sat together on the floor of my apartment for a moment, then I moved away from them to the couch before they could grab me to hug me.

They sat on the floor facing me.

"You weren't supposed to hear all of that," I whispered and looked at my hands.

"You should talk to us more," Rhys chastised. "We shouldn't have had to hear that from you because of a Kitsune spell."

"It's not easy for me to tell you that type of stuff. You guys don't talk to me about things like that," I reminded them.

"We talk to each other," Fox said.

"Still not me," I pointed out.

"Stop trying to change the subject," Deryn said.

"Let's start with point one," Fox said, putting up a finger like he was counting. "Love is not stupid."

"We told you that kids aren't important to us," Rhys frowned, his brow drawing together. "You told us you were going to get your tubes tied, and we were fine with that."

"You say that, but if I told you I decided to have kids, you'd be ecstatic," I snapped.

"Yes, of course we would!" Rhys snapped back. "Having a kid with you would be great."

"See!" I yelled and stood up. "You want kids."

Fox stood between me and Rhys and said, "We want kids, but we are fine not having them as well."

"What brought the kids up all of a sudden?" Deryn asked.

"Lunch," I replied and plopped back down on the couch. "Seeing you with the twins tonight."

"We know that sex has been sparse," Nico said. "We're sorry about that. We have told you that you can take one of us away if you want."

"I can't do that." I shook my head, and my hands fisted.

"Tell us your dream." Deryn reached out and set a hand on my knee.

I sighed and told them the entire dream. They listened silently through it, then all turned to face each other.

"Dhampirs fighting alongside vampires?" Rhys asked.

"That would be a hell of a fight." Deryn growled and shoved a hand through his black hair.

Fox chewed on a lip and I found myself mesmerized by it. "The dream does sort of sound like a premonition," he said.

"It does," Nico agreed with a sigh. He rubbed his temples and murmured something too low for me to hear.

"I don't want you to die," I whispered.

Rhys pulled me off the couch and into the center of them on the floor. They all hugged me, and I sniffled, trying to hold back the tears.

"We don't care how much or how little money you make," Rhys whispered. "You love your job and that is what matters."

"You do contribute to us. You don't see it, but you have helped shape us into better princes just by being our queen," Fox said.

"Ask our fathers," Deryn muttered. "They'll tell you that we've changed because of you and it's something they appreciate."

"Dan's told me that," I admitted with my words muffled as I pressed my face into Nico's chest.

"If you don't want kids, then we won't have kids," Nico said. "We could always adopt."

"Or, we could get a surrogate," Fox suggested.

"I don't know how I feel about a surrogate," I admitted. If someone was going to carry a child by one of them, while we were together, shouldn't it be me?

"You don't need to feel obligated to have a child with any of us," Deryn said. "We won't ever pressure you."

"If you want to get your tubes tied still, we're fine with that," Rhys told me. "We'll go with you to your appointment if you want us there."

"And, you are worthy of us. We aren't worthy of you. You're way more understanding than any of the other girls we've dated. None of them understood our nuances or our quirks," Deryn told me.

"And there wasn't a single girl who we all liked. One of us would bring a girl to meet the others and some of us wouldn't get along with her. We all love you. We all love spending time with you. You're not a rut in the way. You're another friend added to our group. You're our last puzzle piece," Fox said.

"Why am I so emotional?" I asked angrily.

"Nar," Fox said. "He messed with your emotions to get you to open up to us."

"How long will this last?"

I really hated being emotionally vulnerable like this.

"Until tomorrow or the next day," Fox informed me.

Wonderful.

"Are you second-guessing mating with us?" Rhys asked.

"No," I said immediately. "No. I am not second-guessing mating with you four. I want to mate with you. I'm sorry I didn't make it a priority. I hadn't realized how much time had passed until Thor mentioned it today."

"Thor?" Rhys asked. "You saw Thor today?"

"He's helping my dad with some stuff," Deryn explained.

"How has it been two months?" I asked softly.

"You've been so busy with the new game release that you lost track of the days," Nico said and smiled.

"Wait, that means it's March and we missed Valentine's Day?" I asked.

"We never celebrated it before, and since you didn't bring it up, we thought you didn't either," Rhys admitted.

I was the worst girlfriend ever.

"I'm sorry," I whispered. Turning to my right, I threw my arms around Rhys's neck and kissed his cheek. "I'm so sorry."

"You don't need to apologize," Rhys assured me.

"I do. I've been a terrible queen. I've neglected you four."

"That's enough," Nico whispered and pulled me from Rhys's hold. He tilted my chin up to look at him. "We've all been busy and neglecting each other. Why don't we take Saturday and split the day up, so we can each have some alone time with you?"

"You'll only get a few hours with me like that," I reminded him.

"We will take whatever morsels of time we can get with you," he whispered.

"Especially if it's time alone," Fox said.

"We need to make a schedule again and stick to it," Rhys added.

The other three nodded in agreement.

CHAPTER 2

Rhys pushed open the door to his family's house, and I was pulled away by a rambunctious teenage boy.

"Jolie! Come see," Gavin, Rhys's younger brother, said as he dragged me by the hand down the hallway and into a large living room. The furniture looked centuries old, and the room was filled with older dragons. They all looked up as we came in, but Gavin paid them no mind. He pulled me to a set of double doors on the opposite side which led to a balcony where we could see to the town. "Look!" he ordered me with a wide smile.

Gavin's energy was unrivaled, he made even Fox look slow.

I looked out the direction he pointed and saw the town being decorated.

"Is there a festival coming up?" I asked him, admiring the bright teal designs.

"Yes! It's the Night of the Dragon Festival," he said and bounced beside me. "You're coming right? You'll be here?" he asked and looked over at Rhys who was speaking to Emrys.

"I'm not sure," I admitted. "I didn't know there was a festival."

"Rhys!" Gavin called into the other room. "Can she come to the festival? I can stay with her and—"

"I can chaperone," Andras said, hopping down from the balcony above us to land beside me.

"Andras!" I said and smiled. Andras was Rhys's younger brother by a couple of years.

He kissed my cheek and smiled warmly at me. "We've missed you here, Jolie."

"I was here last week," I reminded him with a chuckle.

"A day is too long to go without seeing your lovely face," he murmured in my ear.

"Andras," Rhys growled across the room. "Stop flirting with my queen."

"Not going to happen," he told Rhys with a wide smile. "She's family now and I like watching you get all worked up."

"What happens at this festival?" I asked Andras and was thankful when Emrys distracted Rhys.

"Vendors, games, fireworks—"

"I'm sold!" I said and smiled happily at the two younger siblings.

"I should have known you were the cause of all this raucous," Rhys's mother, Adelaide, said as she entered the room. After giving me one hard glare, she turned and smiled warmly at the others in the room. "Welcome," she greeted them.

Andras draped an arm around my shoulders and Gavin linked his hand with mine, protectively. Their reactions were unconscious for them and it made me feel better.

"I'm alright," I whispered to them and they both stepped away from me. At Christmas, she had said she accepted me, but now she was being cold again. Why?

Emrys walked to me and kissed my cheeks. "Hello, Daughter."

"Father," I replied.

"Come. Walk with me," he ordered.

Rhys started to come, but Emrys held up his hand. "Stay with your mother."

Rhys's lip twitched, but he nodded and stayed in the room. Emrys tucked my hand into the crook of his arm and led me away from the house. "Rhys told me about your dreams."

I sighed. "Of course, he did."

"But, he said you flew yesterday."

I cringed. "Not really. I floated more than flew."

"And?"

"And I fell, like a chick from a nest. I don't know how I didn't break a wing," I admitted to him.

"Why does flying scare you?"

"It's not flying. It's falling."

He nodded, stopping in front of a piano in front of the great room where we stood. This one had the same age-old furniture but looked more lived in and less like a museum. "Then, we need to focus on teaching you to fall properly."

"Come again?" I asked and stopped walking.

"If your fear is falling, then we need to teach you how to prepare for crash landings. We all fall at some point and knowing how to fall is very important."

"Do you think my dreams are premonitions?" I asked.

He shrugged, his eyes darting toward the hallway where the voices suddenly grew louder and laughter flowed down to us. "I'm not a seer. I can't tell you if they are or aren't."

"Should I go see one?"

"I need you to promise me something," he whispered.

"What?" I asked and met his gaze, which seared into mine.

"If I order you to flee, to leave a battle, you must do it. You must promise me that you will flee," he said.

"I can't leave my guards behind." I shook my head, a lump forming in my throat.

"What if leaving will save them?"

"Then I will leave," I agreed.

19

"Then you need to do as I order. If this battle comes to pass, and I tell you to leave, it is because leaving will help your soon-to-be mates. Understand?"

I nodded. "Yes."

"And, please ignore my mate. She's still getting used to seeing Rhys happy with a woman who isn't her. It's a motherly instinct to hate the woman he loves."

I chuckled and leaned my head against his arm as we walked back. "I'm glad you're so accepting of me."

"I told you. It's some weird magic you have over us. All of the kings discussed it. I think that also bothers Addy. She is pulled to you but wants to dislike you. It makes it harder on her."

"I can't control it," I grumbled.

"Do you want to come to the festival?" Emrys asked, squeezing my hand that was still on his arm and led me back to the room where the others were and back toward the balcony again.

I nodded.

He smiled. "Good, because I was going to force you anyway."

I laughed, and he left me on the balcony to go talk with the group inside. Gavin had disappeared during the walk, as had Andras. Emrys and one of the older dragons left the room, going somewhere else in the house. Rhys talked with some of the older dragons, his mother at his side, beaming proudly. No one could mistake the pride that shone in her eyes. How could I prove myself to her? Maybe she thought I was playing with Rhys since I hadn't completed our mating bond?

A dragon roared above me. I jerked my gaze up, then quickly leapt to the side to avoid her claws. The female dragon was a light pink color with red tipped claws and spikes. I had never met her before.

She spun towards me and inhaled.

Shit, she was going to try to burn me.

I leapt over the edge of the balcony and shifted into my

dragon warrior form, which gave me a scaled body and wings. She growled at me and I roared back at her. My new appearance made her hesitate a moment, but then she spewed fire at me.

Jumping up as high as I could, I avoided the fire and saw Rhys being held back by his mother and Mawrth.

Why?

I landed on the female dragon's back and flapped my arms and flared my wings to keep my balance. She turned her head and I used my wings to propel me forward and punched her in the eye.

She bellowed in pain and swiped with her front claws blindly.

I landed and immediately jumped up and punched the tip of her snout. Rhys told me it was super sensitive. Judging by her howling, he hadn't been lying.

Shifting into my full dragon form, I bit into the back of her neck, like Emrys had shown me. She stilled and dropped to her stomach, submitting.

I huffed out a breath and looked back at the balcony and the room. Rhys stood just in front of me on the balcony in his warrior's form, his gorgeous wings flared behind him and murder in his eyes.

Mawrth lay unconscious with his arm bent at an awkward angle. Their mother sat beside him, her eyes wide and unfocused.

"Jolie," Rhys said.

I released the other dragon and reverted back to my human form. My body felt heavy from using so much magic. I jumped down onto the balcony and Rhys wrapped his arms around me and rested his forehead against mine.

"You did well," he whispered.

"Thanks," I said.

The dragon turned into a beautiful woman in her early thirties with wavy pink hair. She bellowed and reached for me. Before she could touch me, Rhys stepped between us and roared. His roar shook the ground beneath my feet and the glass in the doors and windows rattled. I could sense his challenge, but since he directed it at my attacker, it didn't affect me.

She fell to the ground, whimpering and crying.

Andras slipped an arm beneath my legs and lifted me. "Come, Sister," he whispered.

Rhys knelt before the woman and whatever he said to her, she nodded vigorously in return.

"Where are you taking me?" I asked.

"To get some clothes," he whispered, then chuckled.

I glanced down and gulped. I hadn't realized I was naked. Usually, my powers gave me clothes.

"You're drained, so you couldn't make clothes," he explained.

"Rhys—"

"He's fine."

"He hurt Mawrth," I said, glancing at their brother's body as we walked out of the room. The older dragons wore mixed expressions of shock and fear.

"They waited until Father and I were gone from the room. Had I been there, this wouldn't have happened," Andras said, his grip on me tightening.

"What was this?" I asked.

"A test," he said. "Mother wanted to test you."

"She looked upset," I commented. Shocked and disbelief were the emotions I really associated with her expression.

He nodded. "Rhys yelled at her and shoved her away. And, she didn't know you could shift so well."

"So, she's going to hate me even more?" I guessed, hiding my face from the people we past in the hallway.

Andras climbed the stairs and stopped in front of Rhys's bedroom. "I don't know what goes on in her mind." He set me down, checked the room, then held the door for me. "I'll wait here," he promised.

I quickly changed into a spare pair of Rhys's exercise clothes that were kept in the drawer. I had to tie the shirt because it was too big and rolled up the sweats, but they would do.

I inhaled Rhys's scent, which somehow still permeated the room despite him not using it. This was where he'd grown up.

His walls were bare and only two figurines sat on his dresser. One was a dragon and fairy playing. The other was a unicorn. Why did he have these? Had someone given them to him?

Rhys roared, and the house shook. I ran out of the room and Andras stayed by my side as we ran back to the room where we had left Rhys.

Emrys stood over Rhys who was slowly getting to his hands and knees. I started to go to him, but Andras stopped me with a hand on my shoulder.

"I will not apologize," Rhys snarled and stood, facing his father with dragon's eyes.

Emrys growled and shifted into warrior form. He punched Rhys hard enough to make him stumble back a step. Rhys straightened and met Emrys's glare again.

"Apologize!" Emrys roared. I cringed back and Andras hugged me, shielding me slightly with his body.

Their mother stood a few feet away from Rhys and Emrys. Her eyes locked with mine and she bellowed, "You!"

She started to move towards me, but Andras stepped in her path. "You've done enough today," Andras growled at her.

She snarled and slapped him. "I am your mother! Your queen!"

I stepped around Andras and stood toe-to-toe with her. "What kind of mother hires someone to attack their son's queen?"

"You're no queen!" she snapped.

"What are you talking about?" Emrys asked me.

"Nothing," she growled and glared at me. "She's delusional."

"When you and Andras left, a female dragon attacked me. She and Mawrth held Rhys back while I protected myself."

"You're a—" she started.

"I saw it," Andras said. "I came in when Rhys knocked out Mawrth. Mother tried to order him to stay. Her order rebounded, and he shoved her to the side to get to his queen."

"She must prove her worth," she said and sneered.

Emrys dropped his hand from Rhys's neck and marched towards us. I had never seen him so mad. It made me nervous and want to hide behind Andras.

He stopped and spun his mate to face him. "She is our princess. She is your son's queen. She is his mate."

She tried to interrupt, but he didn't let her.

"She doesn't have to prove anything to you. I train her. I keep an eye on her. You have no need to do anything. Rhys may be your favorite, but that doesn't give you the right to treat her so poorly."

"She—"

"Has had to deal with enough shit. I understand that you are threatened by her. I understand that you don't like the pull she has on you. She draws us all. Get over it, or you may lose your son. He will not choose you over her," Emrys growled.

"Jolie," Rhys called.

I walked to him and gingerly touched the red welt on his cheek. "Rhys."

He linked our hands and faced his mother who still looked pissed. She hadn't been cowed at all. "She passed your test. Next time, I will kill whoever comes after her."

Her eyes narrowed to slits. "You wouldn't."

"Anyone who wishes harm upon my queen is my enemy. You should remember that, Mother," Rhys growled.

Wings popped up behind him, and he picked me up before taking to the sky.

We flew in tense silence, then landed in front of our apartment building. The media rushed us, clogging the entrance to the building.

"Princess Jolie, what's it like having four princes as mates?"

"Will you be having children soon?"

"Who hurt Prince Rhys? Was it you?"

Rhys growled, and the media members backed off, but didn't stop their barrage of questions.

I walked into the building and took the elevator to my apartment. Rhys locked my door behind us and stomped to the fridge.

Nico and Fox paused their game to look at us.

"What happened?" Fox asked.

"Mother paid Matilda to attack Jolie," Rhys grumbled while looking in the freezer.

Fox rushed to me, lifted my arms and shirt. "Where are you hurt?"

"I'm not," I snapped.

Rhys popped two frozen pizzas in the oven, then leaned back against the kitchen counter to face us. "She easily defeated Matilda."

"What?" Nico and Fox asked in unison.

I rolled my eyes and sat on the couch opposite them. "I've been getting lessons from Emrys, remember?"

"What else happened?" Fox asked Rhys. "You're way too mad for that to be it."

"Mawrth and Mother tried to hold me back, so I couldn't help Jolie," he explained.

"Is Mawrth alive?" Fox asked softly.

"I broke his arm and a few ribs," Rhys said, his eyes shifting for a moment.

Nico ran a hand through his hair. "Your mom is so crazy."

"Who hit you?" Fox asked Rhys.

"Dad. He thought I had disobeyed Mother and shoved her just because I didn't like her saying negative things about Jolie."

"She said bad things?" I asked, not surprised.

"Andras set him straight, thankfully," Rhys said and sighed. "I was too upset to explain it."

25

"What happened once he got the full story?" Nico asked.

"Emrys yelled at his mate," I answered. "Then Rhys told her he would kill whoever came after me again and they would be his enemy. Add her to my enemy list."

"I had to make sure they understood," Rhys said nonchalantly.

"Can I get a minute alone?" I asked Nico and Fox.

They kissed me on the cheek before leaving the apartment and I locked the door before walking to Rhys. I grabbed his hand and led him to my bedroom, then turned and said, "I know this isn't romantic, but we don't really have time for that."

I pulled his shirt off and slid my hands up his bare chest. Of my four guards, he had the nicest chest.

"You don't have to do this right now," he whispered and rubbed his hands up and down my arms.

"We need to complete our mating bond. We are only partially mated and it's driving you guys crazy," I said. "You are my mate, Rhys. No matter how stubborn and frustrating you can be, I will always love you."

He pressed his forehead to mine and whispered, "I will always love you, too."

I kissed his lips and slid my hands from his chest to the back of his neck, pulling myself closer to him. He broke our kiss, yanked my shirt off and my pants, and carried me to the bed. He jerked the sweats off and leaned over me.

"I'm going to mark you," he whispered and kissed my neck, scraping his teeth gently and making me gasp. "The mark will go around the dragon mark on your shoulder."

He bit my shoulder and magic shocked me through his teeth. I gasped in pain and had to force myself not to pull away. Rhys reached down and rubbed my clit while the magic worked. Distracted, the pain lessened. It had been a week at least since we had sex and I ground against his hand and moaned. He released my shoulder, then kissed me deeply, claiming my mouth with his. He thrust into me and I moaned into his mouth. The connection built as the pressure in my lower body did. He and I orgasmed as the connection snapped into place, making us both cry out.

We collapsed onto the bed together and he pulled me into his arms.

"Finally," he whispered. "You're all mine."

"Well, a quarter yours," I reminded him.

He chuckled. "True."

"Rhys?"

"Hm?" he asked, stroking his fingers up and down my arm.

"Are you really okay with not having kids?" I asked softly.

He rolled onto his side and loomed over me, so he could look into my eyes. "I would love to have a child with you, yes. I would love to see what the two of us created. But, I am also fine not having kids. I understand your worry about not having kids for each of us. Life isn't fair and we would never expect you to carry a child for each of us if you didn't want to. Labor isn't pleasant, and we don't want you to be in pain, even if it would mean bearing children for us. If you bore children for the others, I would love those children like they were my own because they came from you. The choice is completely up to you. I will be fine with whatever decision you make."

I nodded and snuggled into him. "Okay."

CHAPTER 3

Millions of stars shone above me as I slammed to the ground on my back. Air whooshed from my lungs, and I gasped for breath.

"Too slow," Tawny taunted me, her golden hair glowed like fire around her. She always looked ethereal, but when we fought, the elf woman looked even more like a goddess.

"Cheater," I panted and groaned as I rolled onto my hands and knees. "You used magic."

"You have magic too. Use it," she ordered me.

"You alright?" Fox called from the swinging tire he sat on in one of the nearby trees.

"Peachy," I growled and stood. My hair blew forward into my face, and I debated cutting it.

"Hold on," Fox ordered me. He leapt off the tire swing and hurried over. With expert and nimble fingers, he French braided my hair, then used a piece of a plant's vine to secure it. He beamed. "There, now it won't get in your face."

I brushed my lips across his, then faced Tawny again. "Ready."

She snickered, and amusement lit her lavender eyes. "No, you're not."

28

Tapping into my connection with Fox, I channeled his elven powers. The forest came into focus, much sharper than before, and Tawny moved at a slower pace.

I smiled and met her halfway, dodging her punch, and leapt up over her leg sweep.

"Yes!" she shouted and threw a barrage of punches at me. Her smile was radiant and my lips curled to match hers.

She laughed joyously as we fought. Sweat slid down my spine and dampened my hair at the base of my head.

Time disappeared, and I worried I wouldn't be able to keep up, but soon, she raised her hand and stepped back.

"I give," she said. "That was amazing."

I released the powers and fell to my back on the cool grass, staring up at the cloudless night sky. "I'm spent."

Fox lay beside me and unbraided my hair. "That was a huge improvement."

"Finally figured out how to tap into our connection," I admitted.

He nodded. "I felt it."

"I need a shower," I groaned.

"No time," he gasped as he looked at the time on his phone. "Rhys is supposed to be here in two minutes."

Rhys was never late.

"Need an outfit?" Tawny asked.

I nodded. "My body smells, too."

She pulled me up and waved glowing hands at me. The sweat disappeared, my body odor vaporized, and my leggings and tank top were replaced by a flowing elven gown of blue gossamer. The front of the dress was shorter than the back, which gave me freedom of movement and yet still looked gorgeous.

I threw my arms around her and squeezed. "You're amazing!"

"I could have done that," Fox pouted.

Tawny hugged me back, then wiggled her fingers at my face, adding a silver pair of earrings that matched my necklace.

Rhys roared, announcing his approach and landed thirty yards away in his dragon form, but quickly shifted.

Tawny tensed beside me, her mouth a thin line. "I'll see you next week," she whispered and then ran off into the forest.

Her behavior was understandable since she had been attacked by a dragon as a child and still didn't trust them. I wished I could show her their soft side.

Rhys and Fox bumped fists with smiles on their faces. It always warmed my heart to see the friends interact.

Rhys tapped our mating bond to get my attention.

I met his eyes and smiled. Now that we were fully mated, he had calmed down a lot. It was a great relief.

Walking with a bit more sway to my hips than normal, I watched Rhys's eyes shift to his dragon's eyes. I kissed Fox and hugged him. "See you tonight?" I asked.

He nodded. "I'm headed home now."

"Love you," I called as I threw my arms around Rhys's neck.

Rhys picked me up, released wings from his back, and leapt up into the sky. Rhys nuzzled my cheek and said, "I missed you today."

I kissed his cheek and tightened my hold on him. "I missed you too. Guess what?"

"Chicken butt!" he yelled.

I giggled.

He and Fox had spent a lot of time together lately and it had made Rhys more childlike.

"No," I said. "I was able to use elf powers, and Tawny didn't end up tossing me on my back."

"Nice!" he said.

I looked at the approaching dragon's den, and my heart sank. "Do you think she will ever like me? I thought she had grown to like me, at Christmas, but now we're back to square one." There was no need to specify who I meant.

"Yes," he said. "She just needs a couple months."

I didn't believe him, but I stayed silent.

Andras in dragon form suddenly flew down to us, making me shriek.

"Andras!" I snapped and took a stuttering breath. "You startled me."

"You think I would let some random dragon drop down next to us?" Rhys asked with a half-laugh.

He had let Matilda fight me.

His eyebrows furrowed, and fury zoomed down our connection.

Andras chuckled, a wheezing dragon laugh, then made a purring sound at me.

"Thank you," I said, assuming he was complimenting my dress. "An elf woman made it for me."

"How do you always know what we're saying?" Rhys asked.

I shrugged. "Same way I can tell you apart when only dragons should be able to." I wiggled my fingers at him and in an eerie voice said, "Magic!"

He rolled his eyes, and Andras roared with laughter.

We flew over the house where Emrys stood on the porch. He raised his hand, then shifted, and flew after us.

Rhys landed in a grassy area near the town with Emrys and Andras on either side of us. The town was quiet and there were no lights on. What had happened to the decorations? The lanterns? All of the things I had seen just a few nights ago?

After brushing off my dress, I hugged Emrys and then Andras.

"Hello," I said and smiled at them.

"Welcome to the Night of the Dragon Festival!" Emrys announced.

Lights, lanterns, and a huge bonfire roared to life.

I gasped and gawked at the amazing decorations and all of the dragons waiting.

"It's gorgeous!" I yelled.

Gavin ran forward and grabbed my hand, a smile of pure joy on his face. "Come on, Sister!" he shouted.

Rhys nodded once, and I jogged beside Gavin to a vendor selling paper lanterns.

The vendor, a middle-aged man with gray specks in his hair and bright green eyes, bowed to me. "Princess, thank you for coming."

The lanterns ranged from simple floral designs to elegant landscapes painted on them. I took my time admiring them, trying to find one that was just perfect for my first time. The vendor cleared his throat after several moments, making me look up.

He blushed and set a paper lantern on the counter top. It was painted with two dragons flying side by side, soaring through clouds together. They weren't just any dragons, though.

"I hope you don't mind, Princess. I just couldn't get this image out of my mind. It's an image of—"

"Rhys and I flying," I finished for him. A tear slid down my cheek as I stared at the two gorgeous dragons in flight.

Rhys wiped the tear away. "She loves it," he told the vendor. "So much so, that she can't express her gratitude or emotions properly." He handed the vendor some money.

"Can…" I cleared my throat. "Could you paint this again? On a canvas?"

He smiled and nodded, his gray speckled hair bobbing with the movement. "Yes, Your Highness. I'll start on it first thing tomorrow."

I held the lantern up to Rhys. "Isn't it perfect?"

He smiled wide and kissed my cheek. "Yes, you are."

"Are you hungry?" Gavin asked.

I had forgotten he was there. The puppy-like teenager didn't seem to have realized that though. "Yes!" I exclaimed. "Take me to the best vendors!"

Gavin's smile widened, and he took my hand again. More

people bowed to me and I looked at Rhys in question as he trailed after us.

"Now that we're fully mated, you are officially part of us," Rhys explained.

I rolled my eyes. "So, the kings naming me princess and me being your queen, didn't count?"

He shrugged. "Guess not."

Gavin and I ate some fried food from one of the vendors on a bench while watching the dragons enjoying the festival. There were hundreds walking around, all smiling, except one woman.

Gavin stood, moving his body slightly in front of mine. "Mom," he said, trying to pull her focus from me.

Her eyes were locked with mine, and I doubted he could do anything to distract her.

I remained seated and nibbled on my food but tapped Rhys's and my mating bond to draw his attention.

She stopped by Gavin, her eyes still fixed on mine, and said, "You're strange and I don't like that."

"I don't like beating up women who were ordered to attack me because you're too afraid to do it yourself," I said.

Gavin's jaw dropped open and he took a small step away from us.

Her eyes sparkled. "You may dislike me, but at least you finally completed the mating."

I lowered my food. Had that been her goal all along? Had she successfully manipulated me?

I stood. "You had nothing to do with it."

She arched a brow. "Whatever helps you sleep at night, *Daughter.*"

I growled and felt my scales begin to cover me.

She leaned forward and said, "He will always bow to me."

My fist connected with her jaw and I gasped, not having planned it, but the crowd's gasp drowned mine out.

She fell to her hands and knees.

"Don't call me, Daughter, again until you mean it. And, he bows to no one, but me," I hissed at her.

Mawrth landed beside his mother, and his eyes glowed as he looked at me.

Andras landed next to me and glared at Mawrth. "Don't get involved unless you want me to break your other arm."

Adelaide laughed and stood. "You've got spirit. I'm surprised someone with such a terrible past isn't more broken than you are."

"Love heals a lot of things," I told her.

Rhys and Emrys walked over but stopped a short distance away.

"Twenty on Jolie," Emrys said with a smirk.

Adelaide looked at her mate in shock. "You think she can beat me?"

Emrys nodded.

She spun to face me. "I challenge you to a Three Bloods Rite!"

I looked at Andras.

"First to draw blood three times from their opponent wins. No maiming or killing allowed."

I handed Andras my food and smiled viciously. "Challenge accepted."

The crowd cheered.

Rhys held our lantern and smiled at me.

"Why are you happy about this?" I asked angrily.

He walked beside me towards the sand arena. "I have faith you'll win." He leaned closer and whispered, "And I won't bow to anyone, but you."

I smiled and kissed his cheek before turning to Emrys and asking, "Any tips?"

He smirked. "Don't get cut."

I glared at him. "Why do you want us to fight?"

"Because she needs to vent her anger and she hasn't seen your secret weapon."

No. No one except Emrys had seen it.

I glanced at Rhys, then Emrys. "I thought we weren't going to show anyone?"

"You're keeping secrets?" Rhys growled.

I batted my eyelashes. "I leveled up and haven't had a chance to show you my new skill."

"This isn't a game," he growled. "You could have shown me."

"I ordered her not to," Emrys said.

"As my mate, she can tell me anything and ignore your command."

"This was before we fully mated," I explained.

"She drops her left shoulder before using lunging attacks," Andras told me.

I nodded and filed that information away.

Adelaide removed her jacket and stood with her dress tied through her legs and around her waist.

I turned one of my hands into a dragon's talon and used it to cut the back of my dress so it was all one length.

Rhys kissed my cheek then motioned behind him. "Look who just showed up."

Nico, Deryn, and Fox smiled at me from the fence lining the sand arena. I jogged over and kissed each of them. "What are you guys doing here?"

"Rhys invited us," Nico said.

I spun and gaped at him and Emrys. "You planned this?"

Emrys smirked. "No, but we guessed it would happen. There's normally at least a dozen Three Blood Rites at each festival."

"Kick her butt!" Fox cheered.

After another kiss for each of my mates, I went to the center of the ring. Exhaling, I calmed myself like I did before each of my matches with Emrys.

Adelaide snarled at me. "Your pretty dress will look so much better when it's soaking up your blood."

"Talk, talk, talk. Let's go!" I shouted. Opening my connection with all of the guys, I covered myself in scales and roared at her.

She did the same and charged forward.

I dodged her talon hands aimed at my face, dropped down, sliced open her legs with my now werewolf clawed hands, and rolled away.

"First blood!" Gavin announced.

The crowd was split between cheering and booing.

She growled and spun around, dropped her left shoulder, and charged. Andras had warned me, so I easily dodged, but she ducked to avoid my attack. Spinning, she sliced open my shoulder. Cheers and boos sounded.

"Now!" Emrys ordered me.

Creating a magic barrier that she couldn't enter, I closed my eyes and took shallow breaths.

"What is she doing?" someone asked.

"Coward," Adelaide hissed and pounded on my barrier.

Blocking out the sounds, I focused on my change. Dragon's scales because they were the toughest, werewolf teeth and claws because they were the sharpest, elf vision because they saw the best, and mage magic because it was the best for defense and offense. Plus, I harnessed my dragon's size, making myself larger.

The crowd gossiped, and someone screamed when I dropped the barrier and stood to my full height.

"She's huge!" someone screamed.

Adelaide's eyes widened, and she gaped.

"One move and it's over," I said in a frightening voice.

One second, I stood before her, the next, I was across the arena and both of her arms were bleeding.

"I didn't see her move," one of the crowd said.

"What the heck is she?" another asked.

"Holy mother of mana," Nico whispered.

"Did you know she could do that?" Fox yelled at Rhys.

"Jolie is the winner!" Emrys announced and the crowd cheered.

Rhys, Nico, Fox, and Deryn came over to me and then walked around me in a circle.

"She's tapping into all of our powers at once," Nico said, blinking and shaking his head.

"I didn't know that was possible," Deryn whispered, running a hand through his dark hair.

"What do I look like?" I asked, suddenly feeling a little self-conscious.

"Like a goddess," Fox whispered, his eyes wide in appreciation.

Deryn snapped a picture with his phone and smirked.

"Catch me," I gasped, then reverted to my human form and collapsed. My energy was gone, like a candle snuffed out.

Deryn, who stood closest, caught me. "You alright?" he asked, his eyes glowing momentarily in his worry.

I snuggled into him and nodded. "Just takes a lot of energy to do that form."

"Amazing!" Emrys shouted, a huge smile on his face as he walked to me. "That was the best version of that form I've seen yet."

"Maybe their proximity helped," I suggested.

He scratched his chin and nodded slowly. "Possibly."

"Let's find a comfy patch of grass to lie on," Deryn whispered and nuzzled me behind the ear.

"The lanterns," I said and looked at Rhys.

"We still have a bit of time until we launch them," Rhys assured me.

"I'll get some snacks," Fox said and ran off into the crowd with Nico following him a moment later.

Deryn carried me to a small grassy hill, then lay me down beside him, letting me use his bicep as a pillow.

"You were great today," he whispered against my forehead.

"Thanks."

"Do you have plans tomorrow? I thought we could go on a date, just us two," he said.

"I think I'm free. That sounds amazing," I told him, my eyelids drooping lower and lower.

"Rest, my queen. I will guard you," he whispered.

I awoke from my cat nap at the scent of the food Fox and Nico brought over.

"Food," I mumbled sleepily.

"I see she's channeling Rhys in the mornings," Fox teased.

I opened my eyes and sat up, my mates sitting in a circle with me on the grass. "What did I miss?" I asked.

Rhys shrugged. "A few fights, but none involving us."

Fox scooted closer to me and held out a fluffy piece of bread. I broke it apart and ate it slowly. It tasted like buttery clouds.

"How's the crystal coming?" I asked Nico.

He scowled. "It's still not working right."

"Then, maybe I should just get four," I suggested. "I can put two on each side."

"I'm still working on it," Nico said, shaking his head. "Give me a week."

"Okay," I agreed.

Andras sat down in our circle, eating a piece of meat. "How do you feel?" he asked.

"Still tired, but better," I replied.

Gavin landed behind me in dragon form and curled up with his head behind my back. His breath was warm and made me realize how cold I was.

"Gav, can you move your snout closer?" I requested.

He made a purring sound of acknowledgement and did as I asked, then began taking deeper and slower breaths.

I shivered, then his warm breath wrapped around me. "Thank you."

Rhian giggled a few yards away with three male teenage dragons talking to her. Rhys growled and stood.

"Leave her alone," I said with a smile. "They're just talking and we can see them from here."

"They—"

"I got it," Andras said and walked to the group with his hands in his pockets and a deep scowl. I had to admit, it was intimidating.

"Overprotective," I grumbled.

"What did you do today?" Deryn asked Nico.

I leaned my side against Deryn and listened to them discuss their day. Fox continued to feed me food and I ate it while being warmed by Gavin's dragon breath.

"Jolie. Where are you?" a male voice asked.

"Who?"

"I'm near. I'll find you soon," he promised.

I jerked awake, heart pounding. Was it a dream? Who was it? The voice did not sound familiar.

Deryn smoothed back my hair, a frown once again in place. "What is it?"

"I think a dream."

"Of?" Fox asked, his serious face on.

"A guy, saying he was near and would find me."

"Threatening?" Nico asked.

"Someone you know?" Rhys asked.

I shook my head. "I didn't recognize the voice and he said it like he was rescuing me."

"And it wasn't one of your exes?" Deryn asked.

I shook my head.

"It's time!" Emrys announced.

"We'll do a sweep," Deryn told Rhys.

Andras had joined us again at some point and stood too. "I'll go too."

Deryn nodded and he, Nico, Fox, and Andras went off in different directions.

Gavin growled and flew up into the sky to assist.

"It was probably just a dream," I muttered to Rhys. I hated making them worry over nothing.

He pulled me to a stand, handed me our lantern, and said, "Probably, but your safety is important enough to check it out."

I stayed at his side as we moved through the crowd to where Emrys and Adelaide stood. Adelaide wouldn't look at me.

Wonderful.

Emrys lit his lantern and together, he and Adelaide, released it up into the sky.

Rhys blew out a bit of fire to light ours and smiled. "Ready?"

I took one side gently and nodded. Together, we pushed ours up into the sky and watched hundreds of others join it. Watching the lanterns float together like a swarm of firebugs was just as magical as I thought it would be.

Rhys wrapped his arms around me from behind and rested his chin on my shoulder. "I love you."

"I love you, too. Thank you for sharing this with me."

The group rejoined us a few moments later with nothing to report. We stood, watching the lanterns and enjoying a night of fun together.

"Is it going to hurt?" I asked Nico anxiously.

"Just a little," he said and rested his forehead against mine. "Ready?"

"All my life," I whispered.

My heart stuttered as he smirked at me. He was so handsome, and he was all mine.

Nico placed his hand on my heart and I placed mine on his. Wind stirred around us as he pulled out his magic. Using words I didn't understand, he began the spell. His magic swirled from his hand into my chest, then spread down my arm into his chest. Warmth spilled within me and I could feel his emotions. Love. So much love.

"Yes, I can feel your emotions, too," he whispered and smiled at me.

"It still surprises me how much you love me," I whispered back, a tear sliding down my cheek. "I just hope you feel or understand how much I love you."

Our mating bond felt stronger than our bond as queen and guard. It was intense, more intense than Rhys's mating bond with me.

"Why is our bond so strong?" I asked him.

"It takes it a bit to settle. Don't worry, it won't be this strong forever," he assured me.

"Why is the bloodstone giving you trouble?" I asked. "I know others who have multiple mates and have a single bloodstone."

"I think it has to do with our power levels. I'm able to get two of us, but when I add a third, the bloodstone explodes," he explained.

"Explodes!" I screeched. Now I was really glad we hadn't given in a try the night I had given them theirs.

He sighed. "Yeah. We may need to do two for you."

"I'm fine with that," I assured him.

"Will you put them on the same side?"

"Yes."

He nodded. "Okay. I'll get everyone together to finish the two."

"What if these dreams are premonitions?" I asked. I had had the battle dream and dream of the man talking to me every night since the festival.

"Would you let me take a look?" he asked.

"At what?"

"I can use a spell to see your dreams," he said.

"What are the possible repercussions?" Magic was unpredictable and could hurt more than heal at times.

"It could backlash and hurt me, but you won't be hurt."

I stepped out of his arms. "No."

"Jolie—"

"No," I said, sterner. "I won't let you get hurt."

"It's just a possibility," he said, his brows furrowing.

"Why don't we go visit Fox?" I suggested.

He pulled me back into his arms and said, "I've got a better idea."

I smirked, then squealed as he picked me up and carried me to his room.

"Sex isn't required for a mage's mating, but I haven't had you alone in a while," he said. "I shall take my time ravaging you. Then, I'll fuck you senseless."

"Promises, promises," I taunted with a smirk.

He arched a brow, the bedroom door slammed closed, his front door locked, and a ward surrounded us to keep our sounds in.

"Challenge accepted," he growled.

CHAPTER 4

"Plates!" I yelled, urging my clan members to run to the area in the current map we were playing in *Ghost 2* that looked like it had plates on the wall. This map was a small forest and there were strange dogs prowling around. The tamers protected them and attacked us whenever they could.

"Tamer!" Dragonknight yelled.

"Down," Alex advised, letting us know he had killed the tamer.

"Bones," Turbo said.

We all ran towards the area we had designated with that call sign.

My mates had been summoned to a meeting with the four kings. Something urgent had obviously come up, but their fathers hadn't filled them in. That worried me. I was glad that I had fully mated with all four of my mates now. It settled our group and my mates were happy and content now.

"Jo! On your right!" Orphan shouted.

I spun my character and immediately got tossed back by a tamer.

Orphan and Turbo dropped down from a rock that over-looked the spot I was in and pushed the tamer back.

My character stood, no longer dazed. "I'm up," I said.

They killed the tamer and a large chime echoed through the forest.

I groaned and we all said, "Bugs."

Hundreds of knee-high bugs rushed into the forest. Standing back to back, the five of us fired our weapons, lobbed grenades, and used magic to fend off the waves of enemies.

I loved the graphics of the game and reminded myself not to get distracted by the luminescent colored bugs. They looked like a cross between a cockroach and a pug dog, but with a luminescent shell.

We killed the last one and fireworks exploded overhead, announcing our victory.

"Yes!" we yelled. Finally, we had beat that part of the raid, the third of five steps.

My phone rang.

"Be right back," I told the clan and muted my microphone on my headset. "Hello?"

"The kings want to talk to you," Nico said. "Come downstairs and we will pick you up. We're about two minutes away."

"Okay," I agreed, a lump formed in my throat.

"It's nothing bad," he promised.

"Thanks," I replied and hung up. "Guys, I have to go," I said to the clan.

None of them responded to me, still talking to each other.

"Guys!" I said louder.

"Did you see Jo get tossed back?" Dragonknight asked and laughed. The others joined in.

"Yeah, ha ha. Real funny," I said.

No response. I looked at my mic and sighed. I was still muted. I hit the button and said, "I did it again."

"Talked when muted?" Alex guessed.

"Yeah," I admitted.

They all laughed.

"I have to go," I said.

"Bye, Jo!" Dragonknight said.

"Bye," said Alex.

"Later," Turbo said.

"Bye-ee!" yelled Orphan.

I turned off the console, brushed my hair, and checked my armpits for body odor.

Good to go!

Nico leaned against the inside wall of the apartment lobby, messing with something small in his hand.

"What are you playing with?" I asked.

He opened his hand and showed me two bloodstones.

"Are they ready?" I asked.

He nodded and held them out to me. "I just finished adding mine."

I took one and placed it under my eye, just below my cheekbone. It zapped me and then melted into my skin painlessly. I added the second and a surge jolted through our connections, sharpening them.

"Whoa," I whispered.

Nico exhaled. "Well, now we are all official."

"Happy?" I asked.

He smiled and pulled me into a deep kiss before whispering, "Ecstatic."

We walked outside, and the media sent a barrage of questions at us while snapping pictures.

Nico threaded our fingers together and put a barrier around us, silencing the outside noise.

I squeezed his hand in thanks and smiled up at him.

"So, what did you do while we were gone?" he asked.

"Got through the forest part of the raid," I answered.

"Solo?"

I laughed loudly. "No! With my clan."

He smirked. "Fox got through it solo."

I gaped at him. "No way!"

He opened the door of the SUV for me. "I recorded it."

"Hey, gorgeous," Thor greeted me from the driver's seat.

I leaned between the front seats and hugged him. "Hey."

Nico tugged me down beside him with our still joined hands. "When the kings talk to you, I need you to promise to hear them out. Then, think before answering."

"Am I in trouble?" I asked.

He shook his head.

That was a relief.

Thor drove us to an office building in the center of the four territories I had never seen or been to before.

"What's this?" I asked and stayed seated even though Thor already had my door open.

"This is an office we use for meetings in neutral territory," Nico said and climbed out.

Thor looked at me questioningly.

"Something feels off," I whispered. My entire back was tingling.

Nico stood outside my door, next to Thor, and held out his hand. "Come on."

I took his hand, stepped out, and felt a bit better once he put a barrier around the three of us.

The building was ten stories, at least, with lots of windows. It had no distinguishing marks and looked like most of the other buildings down the street we stood on.

Fox waved at me from a window on the third floor, a huge smile on his face. I waved back, then walked inside. The lobby had no attendant, just couches, chairs, and three elevator doors.

Thor pushed the button for the elevators and rocked back and forth on his feet. It was a nervous habit he'd had as a teenager and it made me smile to see him do it still. The elevator opened, and he blocked my view with his body, stepped in, and held the door for Nico and me to enter.

In silence, we stood together in the chrome elevator, watching the arrow move from floor one to floor two to floor three. How old was this elevator not to have digital floor numbers? Was it safe to ride in?

"If we fell three stories in a metal box, would we survive?" I asked Nico.

He chuckled. "This elevator just looks old. It's maintained every month to ensure it's safe. But, yes, I could protect us."

Thor walked out first then nodded for us to follow.

"Why are you acting like this?" Nico asked Thor.

"Jolie said something feels off," Thor frowned, his eyes still shifting down the hall.

Nico looked down at me. "How?"

"My back is tingly, and I feel anxious," I explained.

"We're shielded," he reminded me.

I nodded. "I know."

Thor pulled open a door, and we stepped into an executive board room with the four kings, my other three mates, and Andras.

All eight men stood.

Nico dropped the shield and walked to the side to take a seat next to the other princes.

Dan smiled. "Daughter! So glad you came."

"I had a choice?" I asked and pretended I was headed out.

Thor pulled out the chair that faced the kings and I sat.

"We have a proposition for you," Katar said. "We'd like to offer you a position."

"I have a job," I interrupted.

"Jolie," Nico whispered. "Remember what I asked?"

To hear them out.

"Sorry," I apologized to Katar. "Please, go on."

Emrys took over. "We'd like you to join our council. We haven't had a human on it because most can't, or don't, understand us. You do. You also have some interesting suggestions that we'd like to hear more about."

One of my mates had been talking to them. I looked at them and they all smirked. Maybe all of them had been talking.

"I mentioned your idea about the combined school," Andras said with an excited grin. "I think it's a great idea and wanted to bring it to the council to consider."

"Oh," I said and felt bad for assuming it had been my mates.

"What is your idea for this school?" Emrys asked.

"I think we should open a school, a private school for now, where humans, mages, dragons, elves, and werewolves attend together. They could learn about all of the Others and the Others could learn about the humans and by attending together, they would learn to interact with each other. I was fortunate to have the pack near me and attending school with me. But, here in Jinla, that doesn't happen. Everyone is sectioned off and separated. Since the war is over, I thought it would be a great time to implement it." I looked up at them after saying my piece.

"What ages?" Katar asked, his hand scratching his chin.

"For the trial, I would suggest high school ages because they're easier for you to punish and keep in line. The council would be presented with candidates from each race and they would be vetted before being allowed to go to the school. That way, we wouldn't have someone sneaking in some kid who is actually a plan to make things go wrong. Gavin would be a perfect candidate for attending the school, in my opinion, Emrys," I said.

Emrys nodded. "Gavin would do well at a school like that. It would be good for him to be around other teenagers who aren't dragons. It would give them more of a real-world experience," he agreed.

"There's a lot that would need to be ironed out for this to work," Johann said.

I nodded. "There are a lot of steps to opening an institution like this, but I think it's worth the effort."

"We will begin working on it," Dan said, and the other three kings nodded.

I smiled and felt useful for the first time in a while.

"Back to you joining us," Dan said. "We would pay you and it wouldn't be full time, just once a week for a few hours. Unless, urgent matters come up."

"What would I be required to do?" I asked.

I wasn't against the idea, but I wanted to know what I was getting into.

Johann floated a stack of papers to me while he remained seated. "This is your proposed duty statement. We are willing to make adjustments if you have concerns."

I grabbed the floating papers and reviewed them. It all seemed pretty basic. I would be their fifth member, their tie breaker. I would make decisions and could offer ideas and opinions.

I would be an idiot to refuse.

"What's the pay?" I asked. Knowing them, it would be way too much.

"You'll be compensated at an appropriate rate," Johann said.

"When would I start?" I asked. "If I accept."

"Tonight," Dan said.

"What are the steps?" I asked. A throbbing pain built in my temple and I rubbed at it. What was going on? Where was the pain coming from?

"I, King Daniel of the Werewolves, nominate Jolie Bernardo as human councilor," Dan said loudly.

Magic gathered in the center of the room.

What the heck?

"Votes?" Dan asked.

"Yes," Katar said.

"Yes," Johann said.

"Yes," Emrys said.

"Congratulations, Jolie," Dan boomed.

The magic exploded outwards and punched me in the chest. I gasped and fell backward out of my chair, fighting to breathe.

"Jolie!" several voices yelled.

Everything hurt. I couldn't move.

"What happened? Why did it backfire?" Dan asked.

"That would only happen if—" Johann began, but suddenly everyone was silent and even my mates stopped moving towards me. Everyone stood perfectly still. I blinked at them.

"It would only happen if she weren't human," a deep voice said near me. The owner of the voice bent over me and I stared at a perfect replica of my own eyes. "What's happened to you?" he asked.

"Who are you?" I asked him back from my seated position on the floor.

He pulled me to my feet and I stared at the strange, but beautiful man blocking my mates from me. They were all frozen: the kings, my mates, Andras, and Thor.

"Your memories need restored," the man with my eyes said, drawing my attention back to him. He reached out and tapped behind my ear.

Pain ricocheted in my skull, then the memories came.

Home. Familiar places, people, and things. The memories were in fragments.

There weren't very many of them, since they were only from the time I was born until I was seven years old, but they opened a startling new reality.

My father wasn't the vampire who had raised me. No, he and the old woman had been my foster family. The man standing before me, he was my true father.

"Dad," I gasped.

He smiled and he was even more mesmerizing than I realized originally. "Hello, Jolie. It's time to come home."

Fear struck me at his words. I stepped back from him. "No. You banished me. This is my home."

He looked at my cheek with the bloodstones and then at my chest. "What are these bonds?" He started to reach for them, and I slapped his hand away and stepped back, stumbling over my fallen chair.

"They're my mating bonds!" I snapped. "Don't touch them!" I wouldn't lose the bonds again. Never again.

He looked at the men behind him. "Which of these men think they're worthy of you?"

"Why are you here?" I snapped to get his attention off of them.

The beautiful man, who had come with Dad, held a trident and kept the kings and princes immobilized, but kept casting strange glances at me.

"I made a grave mistake sending you away. It's time for you to return to Atlantis," he said, narrowing his eyes at me.

"Who is this?" Nico asked, barely able to move his lips.

The spell silencing them was wearing off.

"I'm her father," Dad said.

Nico's brows furrowed. "Her dad was a man turned vampire."

"That was her foster family," he explained in a bored tone. "I'm her biological father."

"How did you find me?" I asked.

"I've been tracking you," the beautiful man holding the trident explained. His silver hair was long, reaching down to his waist in a thick braid and his face was angelic. "You heard me talk to you in your dreams, remember? When the magic hit you, we were finally able to pinpoint your location."

"Who are you?" I asked, still confused, despite my memories being back. Memories before you were seven weren't great once you past your twenties.

"Brayden. Your betrothed," he said and smiled. "We were best friends as kids, too. You should remember that now."

"I have mates already," I said sternly.

He shrugged. "What's one more?"

All four of my mates growled, and I agreed with the sentiment.

"I'm sorry, but I don't want any more mates," I told him.

"We're wasting time," Dad said angrily.

"She's ours. You can't take her," Dan growled, his eyes shifting and glowing, but his body still held immobile and holding back his change.

Dad faced him fully. "Jolie isn't human. She's the Princess of the Sirens, and we are separate from you and Jinla."

"Sirens? She's not a siren," Emrys said.

"She's a null," Dad explained. "She can't feed off emotions or sex, but she is alluring. I'm sure you've all felt the pull to her. How she's likeable and her smile warms your heart?"

All eight males' eyes widened.

"Come, or I break your connections and kill them," Dad threatened.

I was fairly certain he wouldn't follow through on the threat, but I didn't want to push him. I didn't want to risk my mates' lives like that. I looked over at them, meeting eyes with each of them and remembering the pain when our bonds were severed last time. I couldn't put them through that again. I couldn't go through that again. Looking at my father, I also knew he had the power to do it. His arms crossed over his chest impatiently.

"Can I at least say goodbye?" I asked, my heart tightening in my chest.

He sighed. "I'm getting soft in my old age. Fine, but Brayden is keeping them frozen, so they don't try to keep you."

I nodded and walked to Thor who was closest and whispered into his ear, "Keep them safe. Don't let them kill themselves."

"Jo, you don't have to go," he whispered.

"I do," I said and sighed. "Please, Tim. Please, try to keep them safe while I'm gone."

I kissed his cheek and then hurried over to Andras and asked him to do the same. I hugged Nico and kissed his lips. "I'll come back," I promised. "I'll come back as soon as I can."

"He's not lying, then?" he asked.

I shook my head. "The memories are mine. I am a siren, but a null, like he said. They banished me because of it, too embarrassed to keep me in the court."

"Why go now?" he asked.

I smirked. "To keep you safe, idiot."

"I love you, Jolie."

I leaned my forehead against his and whispered, "I love you too, Nico."

"Please," Deryn whispered. "Please, don't go. Not again. I can't lose you again."

I hugged him tightly and peppered his face with kisses. "I'll come back. I promise. This isn't goodbye. This is just an unexpected vacation."

"I'll find you," he whispered.

I shook my head. "No, even if you tried, you wouldn't be able to find Atlantis. It's too well hidden. Please, just wait for me. I swear on the moon, I will come back to you."

He kissed me deeply and growled softly. "I love you."

"I love you, too." The tears were getting harder to hold back.

Rhys was glaring at Brayden but dropped his eyes to mine when I stood in front of him. "You sure about this?" he asked.

I nodded. "This isn't a trick. He didn't implant memories. He freed my true memories. I wish I had known. I wish I could have known to warn you."

"How long will you be gone?" he asked.

"I don't know," I admitted. "But, I'll come back as soon as I can. At the very least, I'll send word to you."

I kissed him and rubbed our cheeks together. "Stay safe, Puff. I love you."

"I love you too, Jolie," he whispered, a single tear sliding down his cheek.

"Don't go," Fox whispered. "Don't go. Don't go. Don't go."

"Foxfire," I whispered and hugged him. "I love you. I love you more than chocolate. I love you more than all the chocolate in the world."

"I'll buy you all the chocolate in the world if you stay," he promised, two tears sliding down his cheeks.

"I love you."

"I love you, too."

I faced the kings and bowed to them, sniffling to hold the tears in. "Please, keep my guards and my mates safe while I'm away."

"Jolie, you don't have to do this," Dan said.

"He's right," Johann said. "You don't have to go."

I stepped back to stand beside my father and wiped at the tears on my face. "I wish things were different. I have to go. I have to obey my king."

"We are your kings. You pledged yourself to us," Emrys reminded me.

"I will return," I told them. "But, please, don't hold your breath."

Dad set his hand on my shoulder and Brayden backed up until he was close enough for Dad to set his other hand on his shoulder. "Thank you for taking care of my daughter in my absence," he said and then the room filled with the men I loved most in the world vanished.

CHAPTER 5

The room Dad teleported us to looked nothing like Atlantis. The curtains were cheap, flimsy material, definitely hotel room quality.

"We're just picking up our things," Brayden said.

All four of my mates were freaking out. Anger, fear, and sadness filtered through the bond in a jumble of emotions. I sent as much love and calmness as I could back to them.

I didn't like this situation either, but Dad was much stronger than they knew. He could turn them all against each other. I wouldn't let that happen.

"What am I expected to do when I return? I don't know anything about sirens or our society," I said, clenching my hands into fists. I wanted to his something.

"Brayden will be teaching you on our journey," Dad answered and strode to his luggage. "We must take the train and then a boat—"

"And then the Kraken will pick us up," I finished for him. "I remember that much." *Now.*

My entire life had been a lie. Human? I wasn't human at all.

I realized Dad hadn't answered my question. It seemed like they were trying really hard to keep me in the dark.

"Let's go," Dad ordered us.

Obediently, I followed him with Brayden right behind me. At the reception desk, the receptionist bowed and said, "Safe travels, King Dalton."

He nodded once, and we left the hotel. Why hadn't his arrival been headline news?

Outside the hotel, the media rushed us.

"King Dalton! What are your plans in Jinla?" one reporter asked.

"I came to get my daughter. My business with Jinla is now complete," he answered.

"Princess Jolie, what are you doing here?"

"Are you his daughter?"

"Aren't you human?"

"Where are your guards? The princes?"

"Are you leaving?"

"Princess Jolie?"

"Princess Jolie is unavailable for comment," Brayden said sweetly. A wave of power washed over the media members and immediately, they silenced with huge smiles on their faces.

Sirens were the worst manipulators in the world. They were also excellent liars, one of the many reasons I wasn't looking forward to returning.

"Is there a queen?" I asked Brayden softly.

He shook his head. "You're the only heir."

I hadn't asked about heirs, but that was helpful information to have.

A black SUV pulled up to the curb and before the doors opened, I smelled the passengers.

I ran forward and held my hands up to my dad. "Let me handle this."

His brows furrowed, and he looked around, unsure what I was talking about.

The SUVs driver's side and passenger doors opened, letting Martin and Ezio out.

"Jo," Martin growled and stalked towards me.

Brayden stepped closer, but I pushed him back with a hand to his chest. "Stay out of this," I ordered him.

Ezio and Martin towered over me.

"What is going on?" Martin demanded.

"My memories were sealed," I explained. "I didn't know who I was until he unlocked them just a bit ago."

"Start from the beginning," Martin ordered me.

Ezio stood silently, glaring at Brayden.

"I'm not human. I'm a siren. I'm actually Princess of the Sirens, but I'm a null. Basically, I don't have any siren abilities, so essentially, I'm human. The king, my dad, the guy over there…" I pointed, and Martin glanced before looking back at me. "… banished me from Atlantis because I was a null. They put me with a human family to be raised. Now he's decided he needs me back."

"You didn't know any of this?" Ezio asked, hard eyes filled with fire stared into mine.

"No, I swear."

His eyes softened a moment, then he returned to glaring at Brayden. I was surprised Brayden hadn't spontaneously combusted into flames from the fire in his glare. I knew Ezio would never harm me and even I moved a step away from him.

"And you're just going? You're leaving your mates behind?" Martin snapped.

"I'm saving them," I growled. "If Dad wants to, he could turn this entire city against each other. I won't be gone forever. I'll be back as soon as I can."

"You won't survive long without your mates. You'll go mad," Martin said. "What's your plan?"

"I have to go to Atlantis, find out what's going on, and then fix it so I can come back home."

"Let me come with you," Ezio whispered, moving so close, our arms touched. "Please, let me come to ensure you're safe."

"Princess Jolie will be perfectly safe," Brayden said and reached towards me.

In less time than it took to blink, both Ezio and Martin had shifted into warrior forms and pushed me behind them. Brayden had his trident out and aimed at Ezio.

"Enough!" I snapped. I shoved Ezio and Martin back and exhaled loudly, trying to release some of the nervousness building. "Please, just trust me. I can't let you get hurt. Please keep the princes safe while I'm gone. And, don't even think about coming after me. You won't be able to find me."

"This is insane," Martin growled and reverted back to his human form.

I hugged him and whispered, "I'll be back. I promise."

Ezio pulled me into a hug. "Please, take me with you."

I shook my head. "They won't let me. The guy with the trident is my personal guard. Plus, I can use my mates' powers still. I'm not defenseless. They have no idea what I can do, so I've got the upper hand."

He inhaled at my neck and I pet his head. "'Come home or I'll boil the sea to find you,'" Ezio said. I looked up and he whispered, "My prince asked me to tell you that."

"Tell him to give me three months," I whispered.

"You have one month, max," Martin whispered. "You go any longer than that away from them and you will all go mad. The last thing we need is those four going mad. It will be worse than when your bonds were cut. Insanity is much harder to cure."

I hugged them each again and returned to my dad who looked irritated.

"Are you done now? Can we go?" Dad asked.

I glared at him. "You're the one who showed up unannounced

and is yanking me out of my life. Giving me ten minutes isn't much to ask."

He opened the door of a taxi and waved me in. "After you, Your Highness."

Ignoring his jab, I climbed into the taxi and buckled my belt. Ezio and Martin hadn't gotten into the SUV yet. Martin was on the phone, while Ezio stared at Brayden who also hadn't turned away yet.

"You let anything happen to her and I'll tear your head off," Ezio told him.

"Don't threaten me, dog," Brayden snapped.

"I'm not threatening you. I'm telling you. If you let anything happen to her, I will tear your head off of your body," Ezio said calmly.

"You're in love with her," Brayden realized.

"She's my princess," Ezio growled. "And I will do anything to keep her safe. You should just let me come with you."

Brayden laughed. "Not going to happen."

"Then make sure she stays safe," Ezio said and turned away, showing Brayden his back, and getting into the SUV.

Martin glared at Brayden and then got into the driver's seat.

"You've got some interesting friends," Dad commented.

I decided letting him know they were my ex-boyfriends wasn't necessary at the moment, so I said nothing. Brayden finally got his luggage into the trunk and climbed in the front seat.

"What am I expected to do while I'm back?" I asked Dad, since he was stuck in the backseat of the car with me.

"You're expected to be our princess," he said as though that answered anything.

"What does a siren princess do?" I asked.

"Brayden will explain all of that," he grumbled and faced out the window.

I sighed and leaned my head back against the seat. This was

ridiculous. If Martin was right, I only had one month to get this figured out. Brayden was my only hope in finding out what was going on.

He had said we were best friends, but I didn't remember anyone named Brayden. There were only a few people I interacted with before they banished me. I needed to get him on my side but explain there was no way in hell he was going to become my mate.

The taxi dropped us off at the train station and I wasn't surprised to find yet another group waiting for me. I sighed and said, "Two minutes."

"Aren't you popular?" Brayden growled.

"I'm Princess of the Four Clans," I told him. "Yes, I am popular."

"Were," Dad said. "You *were* their princess."

"No, I still am," I told him and climbed out of the car.

The train station was noisy and there were hundreds of people getting on and off trains. Standing to one side were Declan and Kylan, dragon twins I had dated when I was younger.

"What are you two doing here?" I asked as I approached.

"Who do we have to kill?" Declan asked, looking over my head. His icy killer gaze was scaring people and they gave the twins a wide berth.

"You're not killing anyone," I told him and sighed. This was one of the issues of dating such powerful and bloodthirsty beings. "I have to do this. Why do I have to keep repeating myself?"

"You don't have to do this," Declan said.

"We can take you away right now," Kylan said.

"No, you can't. You would shift and then they'd use their powers to make you attack each other or innocent bystanders. Look, while I'm gone you guys need to get together, all four clans, and do research on sirens. And, keep my mates out of trouble. I'm not weak. I'm not human. Plus, they aren't kidnapping me. This is my biological dad and there's something going on that they need me to help them with. I don't know what it is, but I have to see if I can help them."

"How do you know they need your help?" Kylan asked.

"I just do. Please, trust me."

"Princess," Brayden called. "It's time to go."

"That the asshole who thinks you're going to take him as a mate?" Declan growled, smoke seeping out of his nostrils.

Did everyone know what had happened?

"Yes, but I have no intention of taking anymore mates," I said adamantly.

"Make sure he knows that," Kylan said.

"Hugs and then I've got to go," I told them.

"We'll find you if we need to," Declan promised.

After hugging them, I went to Brayden and followed him onto the train. Getting on the train made me remember my last train trip and the Summit.

"Why aren't you part of the Summit?" I asked Dad as I sat beside him in an empty train car.

He didn't respond.

Pulling out my phone, I sent a quick message to the guys. Atlantis likely didn't get cell reception.

Me: I love you. I'll get this handled as fast as I can. I know you're not happy, I'm not either, but I'm doing this to protect Jinla. Sirens are powerful manipulators and Dad is the strongest siren alive. Or, at least he was before I was banished. I'm the only heir and I have a feeling that's part of why they are bringing me back. I'm safe. I'm still connected to you. I can still use your powers. Please, try to relax. I will come back to you.

Immediately, I got responses.

Rhys: I love you.

Deryn: Tell Trident Douchebag I'll cut him to pieces if he touches you.

Fox: I miss you already.

Nico: I love you, my queen.

Deryn: Love you, baby.

I put my phone in my jacket pocket and closed my eyes with a sigh. Couldn't my life be calm for just a few months?

"Here," Brayden said.

I opened my eyes and accepted the worn leather book he held out to me. There was no title or author name.

"It's basic information on sirens," he said.

I opened it and found handwritten pages inside.

"Did you write this?" I asked.

He nodded. "I knew you would need it, when you finally returned."

His cheeks had a slight pink tint to them and his eyes were focused on his hands.

"Thank you," I said and opened it. I thumbed through the pages, reading snippets, and was surprised to find drawings of animals, plants, and maps of Atlantis.

Dad and Brayden talked, but I tuned them out as I read. There was so much information, but none of it answered the big question.

Dad moved to the back of the train car to take a phone call, leaving me and Brayden alone.

Brayden tilted his head as he looked at me. "You really don't remember me, do you?"

"Sorry," I said and shrugged. "Even with my memories back, I don't remember."

"You and I have been betrothed since we were born. I was the only one allowed to play with you."

"I'm sure our betrothal ended when I was banished, so why didn't you find someone else?" I asked.

"Your banishment was a huge shock to me. No one told me until you were already gone. Even now, I don't understand why they did it. Okay, I do, but—"

"You do?" I asked, interrupting him.

He nodded. "Being a null means, other sirens can manipulate you. You wouldn't be a good queen because others could control you."

That did make sense, but it didn't make it hurt any less.

"Part of me always believed you would be back. Or maybe hoped is the better word. So, I never found a mate."

"Well, now you're free to," I told him with a warm smile.

He scowled.

"Brayden, get us something to eat," Dad ordered him, interrupting Brayden before he could say anything in response.

Brayden left, and Dad faced me with an intense expression. "Who are your mates?"

"The Four Princes of Jinla. Rhys of the dragons, Foxfire of the elves, Nico of the mages, and Deryn of the wolves."

"Four?" he asked. He looked at my chest in silence and it made me uncomfortable. "What are the other four bonds?"

How could he see them?

"I'm their queen," I explained.

His eyes widened. "Which came first?"

"What?"

"Which bond was formed first?"

"Well, technically I joined their warrior bond first since I'm hum…wait. I'm not human though. How come I joined their warrior's bond?"

"You joined their warrior's bond, then they made you their queen and then you mated?" he asked.

I nodded.

"Do you have issues with the four of them being alphas? With them fighting?"

"No. They're all best friends."

He scowled. "What about interactions with other alphas?"

"Huh?" *What was he asking all these questions for?*

"Have other alphas been affected by you?" he asked in a near shout.

"Well, the kings said I make them feel calm, peaceful. That I'm easy to be around," I admitted, trying not to cringe back from his intense gaze.

I had a feeling I knew where this was going, and I did not like it. Not one bit.

Brayden came back with food and Dad said, "Get mad."

Brayden's brows furrowed, then his eyes blazed and his fists clenched. "Why?" he demanded angrily.

Dad turned to me. "Calm him down."

"Dad, I'm a null. Even if I wasn't, you're too powerful for me to defeat."

He just waited expectantly.

"I don't even know what I am supposed to do," I grumbled. Facing Brayden, I ordered, "Calm down."

He scoffed and rolled his eyes at me.

Now, I was mad.

"Calm down!" I snapped.

Brayden's fists opened, and he staggered a step back.

"Try to manipulate me," Dad said.

No, this couldn't be happening!

"This is probably from my elf mate. He can calm people down," I explained.

"Don't calm me then," Dad said.

"King Dalton," Brayden snapped.

"Oh, right. Sorry," Dad said and snapped his fingers, releasing the anger I hadn't been able to.

Brayden sat down and sighed. "That was interesting."

"Get mad," I ordered Dad. Immediately, I knew it wouldn't work.

"You're not really trying," he growled. "Plus, emotions are easier to manipulate if you channel the emotion from yourself."

I clenched my teeth and said, "Anger!"

Dad's body tensed, and he took a deep breath before saying, "Jolie, you're not a null. You're an empath. You control emotions."

I wasn't a null. I wasn't human. I wasn't anything I thought I had been. Everything was so out of control.

"I don't understand," I whispered. "You banished me because I'm a null. But, now you're saying I'm not a null?"

He sighed. "I was a stupid man and I know there's nothing I could do to make up for what I've done. We tested you extensively and you registered as a null. Perhaps your life experiences unlocked your abilities."

"Well, I've had my fair share of traumatic experiences," I grumbled and folded my arms across my chest.

"Why don't you tell me about your past?" Dad suggested.

We did have a long trip ahead of us. "Fine, but you're getting the abridged version," I mumbled.

An hour later, both Dad and Brayden stared in silence at me, Brayden's mouth agape.

"And that was when you kidnapped me," I said, bringing my story to a close.

"I did not kidnap you," Dad snapped.

"You took me against my will. I didn't want to leave my mates, but I knew you would hurt them to get me to comply. If you aren't kidnapping me, then let me go back to them," I said and met his glare.

"You need to come home," Dad said. "End of discussion."

"Why? You keep skirting the issue. Why are you bringing me home now? You show up out of the blue and take me away. You didn't know I was an empath when you grabbed me. So, why?"

"I don't have to explain myself to you," Dad snarled. "You are my daughter, heir to the siren throne. You need to be in our kingdom, not playing around in Jinla."

"I'm not *playing around*. I have a life there. I have friends. I have a job. I have mates," I snapped back.

"None of that matters. You are princess. You are coming home!" Dad yelled.

"If you would just tell me what it is that's causing you trouble,

I could help you come up with a plan before we get back to Atlantis," I said softly, trying to diffuse the tension.

Dad stood and left the train car without another word.

"I'm guessing you aren't going to clue me in either?" I asked Brayden.

Brayden went after Dad.

I sighed and sat down. An empath? I was a fucking empath.

How would the guys take this?

Had I manipulated them? Had that been why they fell so fast for me? Had I manipulated myself? Was that even possible?

I grabbed some of the food and ate in the silence.

Should I call the guys and tell them what I'd found out? How would they react? Would they think I had been lying? Would they treat me differently?

I put my head in my hands and sighed. What was I going to do?

My cell phone rang, and I knew it was the guys before I took it out of my jacket.

Putting on a smile, I answered the video call.

"Hey," I said.

All four came into view, the phone set up in the center of Rhys's kitchen table and the guys lined up in chairs, so I could see them in the phone's field of view.

"What's going on?" Rhys asked, his brows furrowed.

"Um…" I replied and bit my lip.

I needed to tell them.

"I really wish we weren't apart," I whispered and fought against a wave of sadness and loneliness. Tears sprang to my eyes and I blinked them away.

"Jolie," Fox whispered. "Talk to us."

The four of them looked amazing, wearing tank tops and sweatpants. Had they been training? Or working off their frustration from me leaving them?

"My dad just told me I'm not a null," I said, my breathing becoming erratic.

Panic attack. I was having a panic attack. There was no way to stop it, so I just needed to spit out my story.

"I'm not a null. I'm an empath. He thinks I unlocked my powers at some point after one of my traumatic life events. He asked about how our bonds were formed and I think he believes I may have unconsciously manipulated you."

Tears streamed down my face and I forced myself to look at them, so I could see their reactions.

"I didn't mean to manipulate you if I did. I swear. I didn't know about any of this. Even my dad thought I was a null until just a few minutes ago. If I am an empath, I may have manipulated you without realizing it."

"Baby," Deryn whispered.

They didn't look mad. They didn't look upset.

"Baby, you did not manipulate us into loving you. No empath is capable of making someone love them. You may have made us calm down or made us happy, but those just made us fall for you faster," Deryn said.

"You just said I could have made you fall faster," I pointed out, wiping my face with one hand, while the other held the phone.

"You didn't make us fall for you. You just showed us who you are. You showed us how amazing you are," Fox said.

"We aren't in love with you because you used your powers on us," Nico said. "Promise."

"You're sure?" I asked.

All four nodded.

"Have you figured anything else out?" Rhys asked.

I shook my head.

"You have one month," Fox said. "We won't be able to last longer than that."

"I know," I whispered. "Martin told me."

The train door opened.

"I have to go," I whispered.

"Love you," the four of them said.

I stared at my four mates, memorizing the scene to help me get through the next month, and said, "I love you, too."

Before I hung up the phone, I noticed them all glaring at something behind me.

Brayden plopped down beside me and asked, "What did they want so soon?"

"Nothing," I whispered and closed my eyes.

Silence descended, the only sounds coming from the train as it moved along the tracks.

Turning slightly in my seat, I angled myself so Dad and Brayden couldn't see my phone.

Me: Nico, do some research on spells or charms to protect from sirens and empaths.

Nico: Already on it.

Me: Anyway you'd all wait to tell your dads?

Deryn: Too late.

Rhys: Dad said it explains a lot of things.

Me : (

Deryn: <3

Me: Brayden wrote a book with info about sirens. I'm going to try to get some screenshots to you guys.

Rhys: Who's Brayden?

Me: Trident Douche.

Deryn: hehe :)

Rhys: lol

Fox: :0 :0 :0

Nico: smh

Me: Promise you're going to stay out of trouble?

Rhys: Where's the fun in that?

Deryn: We need distractions right now.

Rhys: You're the one who needs to promise to stay out of trouble.

Me: I never seek out trouble.

Fox: No, but it always finds you.
Me: Why was Ezio in Jinla?
Deryn: He came to talk to my dad about something
Me: What?
*Deryn: *shrugs**

Dad and Brayden moved to a pair of seats in the back of the train car.

Perfect.

I quickly snapped pictures of all the important pages in the book and some less important ones, then sent them through the group chat. I skimmed the book for anything else that seemed important.

Royal Mating

That looked important.

Royals must only mate with royals of other clans. Although it is permitted to have multiple mates, it is strongly encouraged to have a single mate only. Should the heir to the throne wish to have multiple mates, all must pass The Gauntlet*. Only those who pass The Gauntlet and prove their worthiness may mate with an heir.
*The Gauntlet is a four-event tournament usually involving a race, survival challenge, quest, and loyalty test.

Me: Guys, look...

I sent them a picture of the page and waited for their responses.

Nico: We're already your mates. It doesn't seem logical to put us through this.
Fox: Have they mentioned it?
Deryn: Sounds fun.
Rhys: We should make our own if they don't want us to do it.
Me: SMH. They haven't said anything, but it makes me nervous.

Nico sent me a message directly, instead of through the group chat.

Nico: Send each page of the book in order directly to me. I'll read through it.

Me: We're almost to the ocean. Once there, the Kraken comes, and I won't be able to contact you.

Nico: Do it quickly then. :)

I obeyed, snapping the pictures as fast as I could and sent them to Nico. I got to the last handwritten page and froze with my finger hovering above the picture button on my phone. It was a note from Brayden to me.

Jolie, I don't know if I'll ever see you again, but if I do, please don't deny me. Please take me as your mate. Things aren't as they seem. I'll explain in private if we ever meet. Your father is ill and you're our only hope. ~B

I snapped the pic and sent to Nico with the caption: *WTF?*

Nico: Stay safe, my queen. Keep your eyes and ears open.

Me, to the group: Love you all

What could this mean? Dad ill? What kind of illness? And, how the heck could I do anything for them?

A minute later, Nico messaged me again.

Nico: Kraken? What happens with the Kraken?

CHAPTER 6

The train stopped and after grabbing the bags, we filtered out of the train with the other passengers. There were a lot of vendors along the pathways, something common in port towns. The scent of sea water was incredibly strong and it brought back a surge of memories.

I closed my eyes and let the memories wash over me.

"Almost home," Brayden whispered in my ear.

"Farther than ever from home," I countered and opened my eyes.

He sighed and continued after Dad. I followed close behind, watching the various people walking around. I stopped at a merchant with bread and purchased two rolls.

"Thank you, ma'am," the merchant said.

"Princess, you should have asked me to purchase it for you," Brayden chastised me.

"I'm perfectly capable of purchasing my own items and taking care of myself," I growled at him and ate half of my roll in one bite.

A boat with the siren royal crest sat at the docks, and I headed for it. The boat was small, since all it had to do was carry us past the next island and out to meet the Kraken.

Three men stood at attention when Dad stepped up to the boat and he waved his hand to dismiss them. They returned to their preparations, but froze when they saw me with Brayden. Then, they all bowed to me.

"Back to work," Brayden ordered while glaring at them until they stopped peering at me.

They obeyed, and Brayden helped me get onto the boat. He led me to a bench on the deck and we sat down.

"How did your mates feel knowing you most likely manipulated them?" Brayden asked, his eyes trained in the distance.

"I didn't manipulate them," I spat. "And, they all agreed that even if I had, it wasn't my fault. Especially, since I thought I was human the whole time."

"What was it like?" he asked, his gaze finally meeting mine.

"What?" I asked, furrowing my brow.

"Being human."

My frown deepened. Because of the curse I had before, it seemed as if trouble had followed me at every turn. That had only changed a little since I met my mates. "Terrifying most of the time, since I was in danger so often."

"When we get back, I'll help you get caught up on current affairs," he said.

I glanced at him and found him staring out at the ocean again. Was this his way of telling me he would answer the questions I had from reading the book?

"Let's go," Dad ordered the crew.

Before we were out of range, I sent one last, "I love you," text to the guys, then watched the men scurrying around the boat.

The boat moved away from the dock and out to sea. It had been so long since I last visited this area of the world. I missed the ocean.

Out in the open waters of the ocean, I felt small and insignificant. It was a reminder that more important things lay out in the world. Seagulls called overhead, and they swooped down as I threw pieces of the leftover roll I didn't finish. My father frowned when I giggled.

We passed the island and people on the beaches waved at us, recognizing our seal. It was nice to see the siren's reputation was still good amongst the people.

Five miles away from the island, the boat came to a stop.

Butterflies fluttered in my stomach. I leapt to my feet and raced to the bow, hands gripping the railing as I waited. The water before us churned and then a huge head surfaced, followed by giant tentacles and eyes. I snapped a picture with my phone, then turned it off. Even with my phone off, I still had our bonds, which relaxed me a bit.

The Kraken looked us over, then his eye stopped on me. He shrieked and one of his tentacles shot out and wrapped around me.

Brayden and the other men drew their weapons, but I shouted, "Stop!"

The men stopped as did the Kraken, holding me in front of one of his eyes, dangling above the ocean.

"He's not going to hurt me," I told Brayden.

"Watch," Dad whispered to him.

I turned back to the Kraken and smiled. "Hello, Pookie."

The Kraken screeched again and pulled me to his head. I lay atop his head and pet him, his skin slick and slimy. Most found it repulsive, but it didn't disgust me. The Kraken blew bubbles in the water and closed his eyes in contentment.

"Pookie?" Brayden asked.

"I let her name him," Dad explained. "I did not think about the fact she was a young girl and that would influence her name choice."

"Pookie, are you going to take us to Atlantis?" I asked, despite already knowing the answer.

Pookie screeched and thrashed his tentacles, making the boat rock.

"Easy," I chastised him.

Dad cleared his throat and Pookie quickly wrapped his tentacles around Dad and Brayden, both holding their luggage in one hand.

Pookie piled us atop his head, then bright light surrounded us, and he dove beneath the water. The light around us acted as a shield, providing us air to breathe and kept the water out.

Down we plunged, the sea animals rushing to flee as Pookie descended. I stared up, watching the sunlight fade until all that remained was Pookie's light. Down and down we went, the temperature dropped as we did, and I wrapped my arms around myself a moment before remembering to use my dragon powers to heat my body up.

"Your eyes!" Brayden gasped.

I looked at him and smiled. "My dragon mate's powers. I can do many things a normal siren can't."

"Can you shift?" Dad asked.

I shrugged and looked away from them, watching as a tiny speck of light below us grew brighter and bigger. My ears popped. This trench was the deepest in the world and protected by Pookie.

If the cold, lack of oxygen, and pressure of the depths didn't kill you, Pookie would.

Miles we traveled down until the beacon I had seen came into our line of sight. Pookie swam farther down and then into a huge cave. Lava flowed at the bottom of the cave, hardening when it got to the end of the line. I stopped using my dragon powers since it was warm enough now. Not far from here was a giant volcano and this was one of a couple offshoots for the excess lava that kept it from erupting.

A light head snagged my attention away from the lava. A hole in the cave had a silver glow surrounding it. It was the portal to Atlantis.

Pookie stopped and the light moved off his head and to the cave floor. I waved to Pookie, then stepped through the portal between Dad and Brayden.

Atlantis had been a bustling city with vibrant colors of plants, grasses, and animals. I had spent hours each day collecting flowers in every hue of the rainbow.

The Atlantis before me now was not what I remembered. It was like they had thrown a monochrome blanket over everything. No flowers grew. The grass was gone and only dirt remained. A few animals skittered about, but at least three-fourths less than my last visit.

I covered my mouth to hold back my gasp, and Brayden looked at me with knowing eyes. Was this what he meant? It did look sick.

Two guards in royal uniforms, deep blue with silver swirls on the shoulder to signify rank, stepped forward and bowed.

"Welcome back, Your Majesty," the guard on the left said. He had three swirls, indicating his rank as Captain of the guards.

"Thank you, Captain. Any news to report?" Dad asked and headed down the dirt path towards our castle. Even the castle looked sickly.

The Captain glanced at me, then stood and followed just behind Dad. "None, Your Majesty."

"Exactly what I wanted to hear," Dad replied.

The second guard fell into step behind Brayden. He looked familiar, but I couldn't pull the memory out and it was too rude to just stare at him. I was certain I knew him, though. Why wasn't the memory there? Dad had given me my memories back.

We stepped into the castle and I had to stop, more memories flooded my mind so quickly, that I couldn't see the present.

Within the memories, I saw times where I played with a young version of Brayden, as well as the guard beside me, Sam.

"Princess?" Sam asked.

"Jolie," Brayden whispered and set his hand on my forearm.

The memories faded, and I gasped for air. Had I been holding my breath?

"I'm okay," I whispered. "Memories overwhelmed me a moment."

Sam's eyes flashed with anger as he looked at Brayden's hand on me, then he turned away to hide it.

"Let's get you to your room," Brayden said and removed his hand.

Dad and the Captain had disappeared into the castle, likely going to Dad's chambers.

Trailing my fingertips along the walls, I took in my home. It was so much more depressing than it had been.

"What happened?" I asked softly.

"Let's get you to your room first," Brayden said.

I turned to Sam. "Sam, where are all the sirens?"

Both he and Brayden tensed, and Brayden spun around to face us. "How do you know his name?"

"He was in the palace a lot and we talked while waiting for our dads to finish meetings," I said.

It wasn't a lie, we had done that, but we had also spent much more time together aside from that. I felt like Brayden couldn't know that for some reason, though. He had said he was the only child *allowed* to play with me.

Brayden stared at Sam, but Sam just stared back with a bored expression. Brayden resumed walking.

"The others don't visit the royal grounds much anymore," Sam said now that Brayden had turned away.

"The merchants don't come?" I asked in disbelief.

Sam shook his head.

"Where are they?" I asked.

"Shelnam," Sam answered.

Shelnam was the town where all their houses were. It made sense to stay there if they didn't want to be in such a drab area. I was going to need to make a trip out there soon, to talk to the people.

Brayden stopped in front of my door. "Your quarters, just as you left them."

He was right, they looked just like they had before I'd been banished. Rainbow colored walls, unicorn bedspread, pink furniture, and stuffed animals everywhere.

"You're dismissed," Brayden told Sam.

Sam looked at me and I nodded once. "You can guard my door," I told him. Sam bowed, then took up a position on the wall opposite my door.

Brayden shut the door, and I made a privacy shield that would keep our conversation private. Brayden's eyes widened at the emergence of the silvery bubble.

"No one will be able to hear us now," I advised him. "Spill, all of it."

He sighed and leaned against the closed door. "Your father is ill. He's been battling it since you left and we think your presence might help cure him."

"Ill how?"

"Dementia," he said.

I plopped on my butt onto the bed and gaped at him. Normally, dementia was a human-only issue, but if it affected an Other, things could get very bad. A siren being affected by it was terrifying. He could use his powers on people without understanding what he was doing. Someone with low level powers wasn't an issue, but my father could put the world under a spell without realizing what he was doing.

"How bad is it?" I asked.

He ran a hand through his hair and sighed. "I've been able to keep him from doing anything too serious, but there have been a few close calls. It's getting progressively worse each week for the past two months. If we can't stop it, the Elders are considering taking extreme measures."

They would have to kill him. Nothing else would work.

"What can I do?"

"Spend time with him, just be happy and by his side. You're our last hope."

"Does he know all of this?"

Brayden nodded. "Yes. He's the one who suggested that bringing you home might help."

Something about that statement didn't ring true.

Maybe Dad wanted to spend his final days with me as his only family left alive. Or, maybe Brayden was lying.

"Why is everything so ugly and cold? Why don't the people come here anymore?"

Even if he had a few episodes, it didn't explain all of this.

"A month after you left, the dementia hit hard. He demanded to know where you were and killed a guard who said you were gone. During a lucid moment, he ordered all the colors destroyed and forbid the merchants from coming on the royal grounds."

"Why?"

"They reminded him of you."

"If you had just told me this, I would have come."

"But you would have brought your mates."

"So?"

"We're trying to keep King Dalton as calm as possible. Having strangers might set him off."

"You're hiding something," I said, realizing it just before I said it.

"I understand that you don't want any other mates, but I think it would be best if we let your father continue under the assumption we are courting."

"I'm not taking any more mates," I said adamantly. I didn't care how sick my father was, I wouldn't take on another mate.

"You and I both understand that, but let's keep it between us."

Part of what he said made sense, but I got the feeling he still held information back from me. I couldn't pinpoint what it was about him, but I didn't trust him.

"Why didn't you come get me sooner?" I asked. "If this started right after I left, you could have gotten me back right away. It's been over twenty fucking years."

"We hoped with time, it would improve. We were wrong, but he had some periods of lucidity that gave us hope. Plus, we couldn't find you. It wasn't until the newspaper with your picture announcing your bonding that we located you as living in Jinla."

"Dad didn't know about my bonds when you got to me," I pointed out.

"He just forgot," he said, truthfully.

"How long are they giving him before they make their decision to kill him?"

"Two weeks," he replied softly.

"Weeks! That's not enough time for me to do anything."

"It's all we have."

I pulled my knees up to my chest and hugged them. Two weeks to try to cure my father's dementia. A father I hadn't seen in over twenty years. I popped our shield and sighed.

"I need someone to teach me how to use my powers. Find someone, today," I ordered him.

He scowled, but bowed and left the room. I waited three minutes past the time he had left before opening my door and peeking outside.

Sam stood on the opposite wall still. His lips turned up in a smirk for just a moment before he turned serious again.

"Get in here," I whispered and held the door open.

He walked in, scowling. "How can I—"

I threw my arms around his shoulders and hugged him. He was a lot bigger than he had been at nine, but he still had the same mischievous gleam in his eyes.

He hugged me back and the tension melted from him. "Jo," he whispered.

I held my finger up, locked the door, then put a privacy shield around us.

"What the fuck is going on, Sam? Give it to me straight."

"You're in trouble, Jo. We're all in trouble," he said.

I could hear the dramatic music in my head and shook it to rid myself of the ridiculousness.

"Spill," I ordered him. "No one can hear us now."

He leaned against my bright pink dresser with his hip and said, "I need to ask something first."

"Fine," I sighed.

"Are you going to mate with Brayden?"

"No, but that stays between us for now. He said we should let Dad keep thinking we are courting."

Sam scoffed and rolled his eyes. "I bet he did."

"Sam," I growled.

He tensed. "Your eyes changed color."

I rubbed my face and sat down on the rainbow rug beneath my feet. Sam did the same. "I have four mates. One wolf, one dragon, one mage, and one elf. I have access to their powers. When I'm mad, my eyes shift sometimes."

"Alphas?" he asked.

"Yes."

He nodded. "You wouldn't be able to settle for less."

"What?"

"You're an alpha amongst the sirens. So, you would need alphas as mates too."

"I answered your question," I reminded him.

"I don't have any proof for what I'm about to say, but I know it's true. Brayden has some type of magic, not siren based. Mage most likely. He is using powers to control the King. He wants to take over Atlantis and he wants you as his mate."

"Why do you think he is controlling Dad?"

"The night before you were banished, King Dalton told the guards to prepare Brayden's things to be removed from the castle. I don't know where he was going to send him, since both of his parents had died the year before and Brayden was only ten at that time. Brayden had a long discussion with King Dalton in the king's chambers, just the two of them. Hours later, King Dalton came out and said to move Brayden to a room closer to him and you were banished the next morning. Brayden hasn't left his side since. King Dalton has lucid moments and I've been privy to them a few times. It's like he comes out of a spell. It's not like dementia."

"Why haven't you told anyone?" I demanded.

"With no proof, I would only endanger my position and then I wouldn't be able to keep an eye on the king."

"Do you know what he has planned?"

If we knew his plan, we could find a way to counter it.

"No. I think he plans to use your father to try to force your hand at mating. He seemed to be planning to have the king killed. I was able to convince the Elders to search for you, finally."

"It was your idea?"

He nodded. "I hoped you might break the spell."

"Why do you think Brayden is after me if you're the reason I'm here?"

"Because once he found out, he made arrangements for The Gauntlet to be prepared for him to participate."

"When?"

"I don't know."

"I won't take him as a mate. What can I do? Can I go to the Elders?"

"Siren law is clear, to be the Princess's mate, they must pass The Gauntlet."

"My mates are in Jinla," I said, my heart beginning to pound. What could I do?

"If they don't pass—"

"Take me to the Elders. I'll see if I can talk sense into them. I understand the law, but I'm clearly an exception since I was banished."

"I didn't think you'd recognize me," Sam admitted, changing the subject.

I smiled. "How could I not recognize my best friend?" My smile faded, and I said, "Brayden told me he was the only one allowed to play with me and that we were best friends."

Sam's expression grew fierce. "Glad your memories came back."

"That's why I believe you," I whispered. "I didn't get all my memories back from Dad and Brayden was lying to me. The rest of my memories came back when I stepped into the castle with you."

His eyebrows furrowed. "This is not good. No. He's more powerful than I thought if he could make King Dalton do that."

I agreed. "Sam, I need to get a message to my mates."

CHAPTER 7

"The Gauntlet will go forward as planned," one of the three Elders said.

Brayden stood on my right. He'd seen me heading out of the castle with Sam and had followed us. Now, I saw a smirk on one corner of his mouth.

"Elders, I already have mates. They won the Summit Tournament for my hand—"

"Then they should have no problem winning another," another Elder said.

My hands clenched into fists at my side. "I was banished. I should be free from these—"

"You are the Princess of the Sirens. And, you are not above the law."

"At least wait until I'm able to get them here so they can participate," I begged.

"You have two weeks until the Gauntlet," the last Elder said.

"Sirs, you're going to allow four alphas to come to Atlantis when the king is in such low health?" Brayden asked, taking a step forward.

"My father will be fine. My mates will cause no trouble," I promised.

"Tamed them?" Brayden asked and smiled.

"They aren't the ones who need tamed," I muttered and turned away, remembering I wasn't supposed to alienate Brayden. I turned back with a smile and said, "Please, Brayden. Help me out? That's what best friends do, right?"

His eyes sparkled and he smiled.

Hook. Line. Sinker.

"Okay," he agreed. "As a favor to my best friend."

I smiled wide, radiating happiness. I watched in disbelief as it spread throughout the room until everyone was smiling.

Whoops.

"I'll get a message to your mates," Brayden said with a warm smile that I would have believed was genuine, had I not smelled his lie. He had no idea I could smell lies.

I smiled back and said, "Thank you." Before I could lose my composure, I turned and Sam fell into step beside me as we walked back towards my room.

"Jolie," Brayden called.

I stopped and turned to him, my smile back in place. "Yes?"

"Will you join me for dinner tonight?" he asked.

"I planned to eat with Dad," I said honestly.

"Ah, well another night then," he said.

I nodded. "For sure."

His smile warmed at that and he turned away.

"I want to see Dad," I told Sam.

"He's in his chambers," Sam said and pushed open the door to the castle.

I put the privacy shield around us as we walked down the hallway. "He isn't going to send word to my mates. I really need you to do it. Can you? Can you get word to them without Brayden finding out? I don't want you to risk yourself."

He smiled and said, "I haven't survived here the past twenty-three years without you just by my good looks."

I laughed and shook my head. "You haven't changed one bit."

He flexed one of his arms. "I've gotten more muscular. "

"I meant your ego," I scoffed.

"Is there anything you'd like me to add to my letter?" he asked me.

"Tell them not to hurt the Kraken and to prepare for fun after all."

"They'll know what that means?" he asked.

I nodded. "They will."

We stopped at Dad's door, and I dropped the shield. "I'll leave you to your time with your father," Sam said and walked back down the hallway.

I knocked on the door, Dad said, "Enter."

I opened the door and peeked my head inside. Dad sat at his desk, looking at some papers there.

"Hey," I said cheerfully and smiled. I locked the door behind me, slid my foot along the doorway to seal it with a ward, then walked to the chair in front of his desk and sat.

He looked up and smiled. "Jolie, I'm happy to see you."

"I thought we could eat dinner together," I explained.

He stood, his posture suddenly rigid. "I don't have time." His hands moved along the top of his desk while he kept his eyes locked with mine.

What was he doing?

His fingers found paper and pen and he wrote something with his eyes still fixed on me. I peeked over and it took all my control not to gasp.

Kill him.

Stepping around the desk, I grabbed the paper as I stood before him, hiding it in my hand. I hugged him and said, "I understand." I spun, the crumpled paper in my hand, and marched out of his chambers.

I would kill Brayden, but first, I needed to learn how to control my powers. The Captain, whose name I still hadn't gotten, approached. His stride was confident and proud as he moved down the hallways of the castle. I didn't remember him from my childhood, which bothered me. Was he a plant by Brayden?

He bowed to me. "Princess Jolie. Can I help you?"

"What's your name?" I asked.

"Stevens."

"Captain Stevens, I'd like to go to Shelnam. Can you arrange transportation?"

His brows furrowed. "Brayden didn't mention you going to Shelnam. Perhaps I should contact him and—"

"Is Brayden Prince of the Sirens?"

"No."

"Am I not Princess?"

"You are."

"Then why do we need to involve Brayden at all?"

"He is your guard and—"

I stepped closer to him and said, "My guards are ten times the Other Brayden is. You've sworn to serve the royal family, have you not, Captain Stevens?"

He swallowed and nodded.

"Then, I suggest you remember who is *actually* part of the royal family."

I spun and marched out of the castle. Captain Stevens followed me, but I had no interest in waiting for someone to get me a horse. I focused and opened my bond with Rhys a bit more. Wings popped from my back, both tipped with a claw.

Captain Stevens gasped and stumbled a step back.

I turned and smiled at him, knowing my eyes were now slitted dragon's eyes. "I'll return shortly."

Crouching first, I leapt up into the air and used my wings to propel me higher. My fear over falling was gone. I couldn't explain, but with all of my memories back, I felt more like myself and the fear was no longer there. I turned towards Shelnam and flapped my wings. Flying was definitely faster. It took me one fourth the time riding would have.

As I flew into Shelnam, I was excited to see color again. Beautiful flowers bloomed along all of the windowsills of every building. The fields beyond were lush and green, like I remembered, and dozens of small creatures in every shade of the rainbow ran about.

The merchants and citizens froze when they saw me. I minimized my link with Rhys and let my wings disappear.

An old woman, bent with age, hobbled towards me with a cane in one hand. "Princess?" she asked.

I nodded.

The town erupted in cheers and my name being yelled. Children ran up to me, wide smiles on their faces.

"Who is in charge currently?" I asked.

"I am," a tall man with cerulean eyes, tattoos covering his arms, and shaggy brown hair said as he approached. He had a warm smile and I recognized him immediately.

"Colton!" I yelled and rushed to him.

He opened his arms and embraced me. "Jo," he whispered. "You're all grown up."

I tilted my head back to look up at him, well over a head taller than me, possibly taller than Rhys. "So did you."

He touched the bloodstones below my eye. "Mated?"

I nodded and stepped back from him, so I didn't have to tilt my head so much. "I need to talk to you."

All happiness fizzled out of him and he said, "Yes, we have much to discuss."

"First, I need food," I told him.

He smirked and gestured at a building to the left. It had a simple sign which had a drawing of a bowl with steam on it. Mr. Bloomswort and his wife had owned it when I was last here.

Colton pushed open the door and I walked in, inhaling the familiar aromas of spices and seafood. It was empty, which was good because I needed to talk to Colton privately.

Mr. Bloomswort hobbled from the back, a bit grayer than I remembered, but not much different. His eyes widened and he bowed. "Princess."

I hurried to him and hugged him. "No bowing, sir."

He patted my cheek fondly. "It's good to see you."

"She's come for food," Colton told him.

"Coming right up! Take a seat," Mr. Bloomswort said and went back to the kitchen.

The tavern looked exactly the same, even the same tables.

"You look good, Jo," Colton commented.

I looked up and smiled. "Thanks. So do you."

"What are you doing back? I thought you were banished?"

"It's sort of complicated," I said and sighed. "And I'm not sure which story to believe."

"He's very powerful," Colton said.

"Who?"

He smirked. "Your betrothed."

I pretended to gag, and Colton roared with laughter.

"Shit is so complicated," I told him.

"I can imagine. I've been trying to keep the citizens out of it all, which basically equated to us not leaving this town."

"Thank you, for keeping them safe," I whispered.

"Jo, he's not just a siren. He uses magic unlike any I've seen before," Colton whispered.

I nodded. "He's controlling my dad."

Colton sighed and ran a hand through his already disheveled hair. "Shit. I thought he was, but hoped it really was dementia."

Mr. Bloomswort brought out an appetizer of oysters, then went back to the kitchen.

I ate one, as did Colton.

"What are you going to do?" Colton asked.

"Wait for the cavalry to arrive," I mumbled.

"Cavalry?"

"They're making my mates participate in the Gauntlet."

"But, you became mates while banished. They shouldn't have to participate."

"I know!" I said and groaned. "I think he's got the Elders under his control too. Or at least, mostly."

"So, your mates are coming here?" Colton asked.

I nodded.

"And you think they can defeat him?"

I sighed and ate another oyster. "Yes, but I'd like to be the one to do it. If I could be sure I could defeat him alone, I would do it before they arrived. However, I know better and will wait for them to back me up."

"Will they be able to pass the Gauntlet?"

I laughed. "They'll pass easily. They'll probably play around to have more fun during it."

"What can I do?" Colton asked. "You didn't come here to see me."

"No, but it was a nice surprise to find you here," I said and smiled at him. "I need a teacher."

"A teacher? In what? You're a null."

I smirked. "Nope, I'm an empath."

His jaw dropped. "Oh, fuck."

"What?" I asked, my brows furrowing.

"Do you know anything about empaths?"

"Only what Trident Douche told me," I said, using Deryn's nickname for Brayden.

Colton laughed, then said, "Wait here. I'll get someone who can teach you."

I nodded and watched him leave. Nico would have yelled at me for being so trusting of Colton. I couldn't explain it, but I just *knew* he was on my side. Maybe it was an empath ability.

"Here you go," Mr. Bloomswort said and set a platter of fish tacos on the table. "Want some water?"

I nodded. "Yes, please."

I ate all of the tacos and drained my water before Colton returned. He came in, then held the door for the woman he brought with him. The woman was so tall, she had to duck to step through the doorway. I'd forgotten that most sirens were tall. Somehow, I'd gotten the short stick.

Though she always had been a tall kid, she was no longer lanky, but curvy and gorgeous now. She had dark eyes, dark hair, and a rack that made me feel inferior for a moment.

"Jojo!" she said, smiling.

"Leona," I said and stood.

She hugged me, and I hugged her back.

"You two hungry?" Mr. Bloomswort asked.

"Yes, sir!" Leona boomed, releasing me and sitting at my table.

"I thought you were getting me a teacher?" I asked Colton.

Leona frowned, then stuck her lip out in a pout. "I'm not good enough for you?"

"You?" I asked. "You're an empath?"

All three sirens in the room shushed me.

"That's not publicly known," Leona explained.

Well, this trip just kept throwing surprise after surprise at me.

Leona eyed me. "I'm pretty shocked you're an empath, too. I never even got a hint of it from you when we were kids."

"Probably because you spent most of the time trying to catch the boys," I teased.

"While Colton was trying to look up skirts at all the girls' underwear," she accused.

"I'd ask about your underwear, but I see the bloodstones," he said and sighed dramatically.

"I'd have to be wearing some to comment," I said and winked.

He groaned and clutched at his chest, flailing backwards

dramatically. He sat back up and asked, "Would you be interested in a third mate, possibly?"

I smirked. "I have four already."

Leona and Colton blinked in shocked silence.

"You think they can pass the Gauntlet?" Mr. Bloomswort asked as he set fried fish nuggets and calamari on the table.

I nodded. "They enjoy challenges."

"Explains why they ended up with you then," Colton teased me.

I threw a piece of calamari at him, which he caught and ate with a smile on his face.

"You see Sam?" Leona asked.

I nodded. "He's off on an errand for me."

"So, what do you know about empaths?" Leona asked while eating fish nuggets.

I set the book Brayden had given me on the table and opened it to the page on empaths. "This is all I know."

Leona and Colton inspected the book and Colton asked, "Who wrote this?"

"Trident Douche."

Leona looked at me with a quirked brow, then burst into laughter. "Brayden!" he gasped and pounded the table with his fist as he continued laughing.

Colton shook his head as he read it. "He doesn't know about empaths. The other info is right, for the most part, but not the stuff about empaths."

Leona pulled a pen from her pants pocket and scribbled out some information Brayden had written, then wrote a full page of notes. I tried to read it, but she tore a blank page from the back of the book and continued writing information down.

"Wouldn't it be easier just to give me a book that is already written?" I asked.

"They don't exist. All empath books were burned decades

before we were born. It is now past down from empath to empath verbally," Leona explained.

"Why?"

"So outsiders won't find out what we can really do. If they found out, they would capture us and make us work for them," Leona said.

"Why are you writing it down for me, then?" I asked.

She smiled. "You're my princess. Who better to break tradition for?"

"Will you also teach me?"

She nodded, writing furiously. "Trident Douche is likely on his way here. I'm giving you what I can, so you can read and prepare for our training session tomorrow."

"Where am I supposed to meet you?" I asked.

"My house," Colton said. "Same place I grew up in, you remember?"

I nodded.

"Tomorrow, after breakfast," Leona said. "Read this all tonight and prepare mentally. Okay?"

"Okay," I agreed and felt my nerves building again. I really wished the guys were here.

Leona closed the book with the new pages inside and gave it back to me. I tucked it into my jacket, glad for its small size.

Not even a minute later, Brayden walked in. He glared at Leona and Colton's backs before walking to me with a smile. "Jolie, you should have let me know you wanted to visit. I was worried something had happened when I couldn't find you. And Captain Stevens was shouting nonsense about you having wings."

I pulled my wings out behind me, fanning them as far open as they would go. "It wasn't nonsense."

All present stared at my dragon wings with wide eyes.

"Plus, I wanted to visit with some of the townspeople I knew from when I lived here. Despite you being my best friend…"

Colton and Leona's eyes hardened, and their jaws clenched.

"...I did have a few others I played with. Leona and Colton were two of them."

Brayden scowled at the backs of the two sirens, who hadn't bothered to acknowledge him.

"I didn't know you played with the commoners," Brayden said.

"There's a lot you don't know about me," I said with a pleasant smile. "It has been over twenty years since we last saw each other."

"True," he said and smiled warmly, "which is all the more reason for us to get to know each other again."

Colton tensed, and I kicked his shin under the table while never breaking eye contact with Brayden. "Yes, we should. Let's meet for breakfast tomorrow," I suggested.

His smug smile was aimed at Leona and Colton who couldn't see it. "Sounds great," he said.

I batted my eyelashes. "Could you pay for my food? I don't have any currency."

Brayden looked at the plates. "You ate all of that?"

"I burn a lot of energy with my double connection to the four alphas," I said, then stood and patted my flat stomach. "I should lay off, so I don't get fat."

"You look perfect," Brayden said with a leering smile.

I never wanted to gag so much just from a look before. I held my smile in place while Colton and Leona avoided eye contact.

Brayden put the money down, golden coins with a clam stamped on them, then pulled open the door for me.

I hugged my two friends, tucked my wings in to get out the door, then winked at Brayden. "Race you home." Immediately, I flew up into the sky and raced to the castle. I found a maid and asked her to fill my tub with warm water, so I could take a bath. Then, I locked my door and secured it with a ward, just to be sure. Safe, I slid into the warm water and began reading Leona's notes.

CHAPTER 8

I survived breakfast with Brayden, managing not to throw up despite his lewd glances and comments, then hurried back to my room. I needed to get to Shelnam without Brayden finding out.

How?

Pacing back and forth, I tried to think of a plan. I could turn into a wolf, but there weren't wolves in Atlantis, so I'd get a lot of attention. Same problem with a dragon and even a fox. And, I hadn't tried turning into a fox yet anyway.

Nico hadn't taught me an invisibility spell, so that wasn't a possibility either.

I didn't know the staff or whose side they were on, so trying to use them wasn't a great option. I wished Sam was back.

I tapped my bonds with each of my mates and they tapped them back. At least they were okay, for now. While I felt mostly certain they could pass the Gauntlet, I was a little worried. I knew Brayden would participate and he'd cheat however he could.

I should just kill him before the Gauntlet even started. To do that, I needed to get to Leona for my lessons.

Screw it, I'd fly there again and if Brayden tried to stop me, I would kill him. This was my home, my kingdom, and I wouldn't let him back me into a corner.

I put the book in a bag and marched determinedly out of the castle. A few guards looked at me, but none tried to stop me. I flew as fast as I could and landed on the far side of town to avoid as many townspeople as I could. I knocked twice on Colton's door, then pushed it open.

Colton and Leona sat at the dining table with papers scattered across its top.

The house hadn't changed, except all of the pictures save for one were gone. He still had the same dull brown couch, the same seashell chandelier, and the same picture of four dirty, smiling kids, hanging on the ice box. I put up a ward, then walked past Leona and Colton to the ice box. Sam, me, Leona, and Colton stood together, all covered in mud, and smiling like idiots.

"You remember that day?" Colton asked.

I nodded. "It was my last day here." Not that we had known that at the time.

"We'd played for hours in that muddy creek," Leona said and chuckled.

Something small and shiny in the background caught my eye. I squinted and leaned closer, then used Fox's power to enhance my eyesight.

There, in the background of our picture stood Brayden, glaring at us with shining eyes.

"Oh, shit," I whispered. I pulled the picture down and set it on the table, atop some of their papers. "Look."

"What?" Leona asked.

"We see it every day," Colton said.

I pointed at Brayden. "Brayden with glowing eyes."

They leaned forward and then Colton grabbed a magnifying glass and they both cussed.

"Do you think he is the reason I was banished? Sam thought so, but could it be because of him?" I asked softly.

"If so, why let you come back now?" Leona asked.

Suddenly, it clicked. "Because he can't claim the throne unless we're mates," I whispered. "He's going to go after my mates. I know he is."

I started to head for the door, but Leona stopped me. "We need to train first. You're a loose cannon right now."

"He's going to kill them!" I shouted.

"You said they're strong, right?" Colton asked.

I clenched my jaw, but replied, "Yes."

"Just give me a couple of days. Colton and I will come with you afterwards to help," Leona promised.

I checked the bonds, and everything felt fine. "Okay," I agreed.

"You read my notes?" Leona asked.

"Yes." I didn't understand all of it, but I'd read it all.

"So, we can sense emotions, including sensing when someone is using a false emotion to hide their true emotions. We can also manipulate other beings emotions."

"Just like sirens," I commented.

"Yes, sirens can manipulate emotions, but they can't sense emotions. Empaths can, depending on their power level, manipulate more than one being at a time. One more thing we can do that sirens can't? Manipulate our own emotions to empower ourselves."

"Really? That would have been nice to know all these years," I said.

"Your ultimate power though, is addiction," Colton said

"What?" I asked.

"People crave happiness. Generally, empaths are happy people and people want to be around us. They will crave happiness like a drug because being happy releases chemicals in your brain that drugs do and, they end up craving you," Leona said.

"How do I prevent someone from being addicted?" I asked.

"You have to lock down your powers. It sucks, but it's the only way. Luckily, it's not hard to lock them down," Leona explained.

"Okay, none of this sounds terrifying, though. Colton made it seem like I was going to self-destruct."

Leona smirked. "Because I haven't told you our ultimate weapon. Mind manipulation."

"Like sirens?"

He smiled wide. "Better. We can make people see whatever we want them to."

"Hallucinations?"

She nodded. "And I think you're powerful enough to pull it off on a mass scale."

My eyes widened. "So, I could make a group of people think they're seeing one thing, while another is happening?"

Leona and Colton nodded.

"Blue rupis," I whispered.

"What does that mean?" Colton asked.

I gaped at him a moment, then remembered they didn't have internet or electronics. They all made a trip to the mainland at least once in their lives, but they couldn't use any of that stuff here. "Oh, guys. I forgot how sheltered you are here!"

"We're not sheltered," Colton scoffed.

"You're missing out on hundreds of video games! We've got to figure out how to get internet down here," I said, considering how we could possibly accomplish it.

"I think we have more pressing matters to attend to right now," Leona said.

I sighed and rubbed my face with both hands. "You're right. Teach me everything."

We made it four hours with no distractions, then my stomach wouldn't shut up. After a quick meal at Mr. Bloomswort's tavern, we returned to do more training.

My training consisted of me trying and failing to manipulate Colton's emotions. I did figure out how to shut down my powers, which was a huge relief to everyone. Five more hours of training left me mentally and physically exhausted. I kept nodding off and Leona decided to stop the lessons for the day.

"I haven't learned anything," I argued, trying to sit up with arms made of lead.

Colton pushed me down on the couch and shook his head. "You're done for the day. Go to sleep. We'll stay here and make sure Trident Douche doesn't show up."

Leona draped a blanket over me, then she and Colton returned to the kitchen table to go over the papers they'd been looking at when I arrived. I hadn't even thought to ask about them.

"BABY, OPEN YOUR EYES," RHYS WHISPERED.

"Rhys?" I asked and opened my eyes. I stood in a dark room with no furniture and no windows. There was no light source, yet I could see. Rhys, Deryn, Fox, and Nico sat in front of me.

"What's going on?" Nico asked. "You used a lot of power today."

"Training with my new powers," I explained. "Wait, where are we?"

"You pulled us into a dream world with you," Nico explained.

"Yes!" I yelled. "Finally, I did something with my empath powers."

"My queen, focus. What's going on?" Fox asked.

Uh oh, serious Fox was here.

"Trident Douche isn't just a siren. He has other abilities. He is controlling my dad. Possibly others too. I think, I don't have proof, but I think he's the reason I got banished."

Since this was my dreamscape, I pulled up the picture and made it poster sized for the guys to easily see it. It appeared in my hands and I held it out to them.

"That's me, Colton, Sam, and Leona," I explained. "That angry boy in the back is Trident Douche. This was the day before I was banished. I think he started controlling my dad then."

"He's packing some serious power then," Nico said.

"If he banished me, but now brought me back, it must be because he can't get the throne without becoming my mate."

All four growled.

"I think he plans to kill you," I said and swallowed. "Sam is on his way to get you. They're going to make you participate in the Gauntlet."

"Challenge accepted!" Deryn yelled and the other three smiled.

"Focus!" I snapped. "He won't want you to make it. I don't know what kind of powers he has. I'd tell you to stay away and let me kill him, but—"

"You know we won't listen," Rhys said.

"That, and I would prefer to have you as backup," I replied.

"Are you safe?" Fox asked.

"I think so," I said.

"Can we trust Sam?" Deryn asked.

I nodded. "When you get to the Kraken, call him 'Pookie' and open the bonds with me. He should sense it and let you down with Sam by your side."

"Pookie?" Nico asked with an arched eyebrow.

"I was five!" I snapped.

"You named him?" Fox asked.

I nodded.

Rhys walked to me and rested his hand on my cheek. I leaned into it. "Baby, please stay safe until we get there."

"I'll try my best," I promised. "I need you here in two weeks, no later."

They nodded in understanding, then took turns kissing me. I didn't want to end the dream, but felt it crumbling around the edges.

"I love you," I whispered.

They bowed. "Love you, too," they said in unison.

Leona, Colton, and I sat in Mr. Bloomswort's tavern,

eating and chatting, when Brayden and Captain Stevens burst in with a few guards behind them.

"Arrest them," Brayden ordered the guards.

I stepped into their path. "On what charges?"

"Kidnapping the princess," Brayden said.

I folded my arms across my chest. "No one kidnapped me."

Captain Stevens tried to move around me, but I stepped into his path again. "I order you to leave this establishment at once!" I shouted.

The guards, Brayden, and Captain Stevens spun and walked out.

"Whoops," I whispered to Leona and Colton.

We walked out and Brayden glared at us. "Where did you learn to do that?"

"I've always been able to," I lied.

He snarled. "Arrest them, now."

I had had enough of his shit. I shifted into my wolf warrior form and growled loudly. "Take one more step and I'll kill all of you!"

Everyone froze and gaped at me. Merchants, townspeople, guards, even my friends stared.

"I am Princess Jolie of the Sirens, and I am heir to the throne! Guards, arrest Brayden and take him to the dungeons."

They turned, but Brayden dodged them, then ran to me. I tried to slice him with my claws, but the bastard was nimble and he avoided them.

"No!" Leona yelled.

Brayden touched my head and he filled it with his power. Nothing existed, but Brayden.

He was a god, no *the* god! I should bow to him and...

Four golden lights pierced the haze in my head.

"No!" I screamed and clutched at my head.

"You're mine," Brayden whispered, a cool hand touching my forehead.

"Jo!" Colton yelled, but his yell was cut off by the sound of flesh hitting flesh and his breath whooshed from his lungs.

"Stand," Brayden ordered me.

I obeyed. The little fucker thought he had complete control over me. He was wrong.

I met his eyes, then slammed my knee into his balls as hard as I could. He gasped and clutched himself. I punched him in the face with dragon scale covered hands.

He stumbled and fell onto his butt, his eyes wide with fear.

I shifted into my dragon form and roared. Arching my neck, I inhaled to shoot fire and destroy Brayden.

Cold water splashed against my face, making me gasp and open my eyes.

Brayden stood before me, a smug smile on his face. We weren't in the town anymore. Stone floors, iron shackles on my wrist and ankles, and pitiful moaning all pointed to me being in the dungeon.

"How?" I asked weakly. My arms and legs were chained to the wall, preventing me from choking his stupid neck.

"I took control of Leona. I always thought she was an empath, but couldn't be sure until you helped me confirm it today," Brayden said.

"I'm going to kill you. I don't know what you are, but I'm going to rip your head from your body and burn you until you're nothing more than ash!" I screamed.

He chuckled. "You've always been a spitfire. Sadly, you can't fight me this time."

He set his hands on my face, from temple to jaw on each side, and began to shove his power into my head again.

I screamed and thrashed, but I couldn't stop him. He was right, I was too weak to fight him. I slammed my bonds closed, just in case he could get to the guys through them.

"I'm sorry," Leona whispered somewhere nearby. "I'm so sorry, Jojo."

I FED BRAYDEN ANOTHER STRAWBERRY, THEN ATE ONE MYSELF. WE sat in the royal gardens, now just dirt with a pond of silver fish.

Something wasn't right. I couldn't fully understand what it was, but I just knew something wasn't right.

Brayden said we were betrothed and destined to be mates, to rule Atlantis together. Yet, I had two bloodstones beneath my eye. One only got bloodstones when they were mated. So, that had to mean I had mates. But, I didn't remember having mates. I couldn't feel them. I couldn't sense anything. If I had mates, where were they? Why was I with Brayden if I had other mates? And, shouldn't they be participating in the Gauntlet?

So, why did I have bloodstones if I didn't have mates?

"You keep getting sidetracked and spacing off," Brayden whispered, rubbing a fingertip down my cheek. "What are you thinking about?"

"It's so quiet here," I said to change topics. "I miss the festivals."

"You want a festival?" he asked.

I shrugged. "It's been so long since I've been to one. I remember how fun they were as a kid. Isn't there a holiday coming up? A festival soon that we could participate in?"

"No, but we could hold a festival once the Gauntlet is over," he suggested.

"If you win," I said. "I don't think you'll want to have a festival if you don't win."

He didn't seem to hear me.

"What do you want to do today?" I asked him.

"I have to go to the arena today," he said and stroked a finger down my arm.

"Can I come?" I asked and scooted closer to him. "I don't want to be away from you."

He smiled and cupped my cheek. "Kiss me and you can."

I blushed and turned away. "You know the law. You can't be my mate until you win the Gauntlet."

His smile disappeared, but it quickly returned. "You're right."

"So, can I go?" I asked and leaned my head on his shoulder.

"Not today, love. Why don't you find the seamstress to have her make a dress for the day of the Gauntlet?" he suggested and stood.

I pouted and stood too. "Okay."

He pulled me into a hug and kissed the top of my head. "Don't worry, I won't be gone long."

After walking me back to my room, he left to go on his errand. I flagged down a maid and asked her to fetch the seamstress.

The seamstress arrived shortly thereafter. "How can I assist you, Princess Jolie?" She was an old woman with leathered skin and shoulder length grey hair.

"I need a dress for the Gauntlet," I explained. "It needs to be beautiful, but also something I can maneuver in."

"Maneuver, Princess?" she asked.

"Loose around my legs and a high slit on at least one side," I explained.

"Color preference?"

"Dark blue," I said, knowing it was a color that men said I looked good in. A memory tugged at the edge of my mind, but I couldn't access it.

She nodded and pulled out a measuring tape, immediately getting to work. Once she was done with my measurements, she left to start making my dress.

Four simultaneous taps at my mental wall made me gasp in shock.

"Princess Jolie?" a young guard called through the door.

"You're needed outside," he said, his voice shaking with nervousness.

A roar shook the castle and I hurried out to the guard. "What is it?" I asked him.

"Hurry," was all he said before turning and sprinting down the hallway.

I followed, running alongside him out of the side door to the courtyard. Four males stood side by side, facing Brayden with murder in their eyes.

"Where is she?" the werewolf in warrior form asked.

"She is not—" Brayden began, but I hurried to his side.

"What's the meaning of this?" I asked angrily.

"Jolie." All four males breathed a sigh of relief.

"You need to go back inside," Brayden told me. "It's not safe for you here."

I looked at him and scoffed. "I am Princess here, not you." Facing the four newcomers who were scowling again, I asked, "What do you want?"

"Jolie, what's wrong with you? It's us," the short, muscular elf said.

A guard stepped out from behind them and said, "These are the guests who will be participating in the Gauntlet."

I looked more closely at the men. They were all very handsome. And, they were all definitely alphas. They would make for decent mates, if they passed the Gauntlet.

I nodded. "Your rooms are prepared and waiting for you. If you'll follow me, I'll—"

"What did you do!" the dragon yelled at Brayden.

Brayden smiled smugly. "Jolie, come here," he ordered me.

I scowled but walked to his side. I did not like to be ordered around and he knew that. He draped an arm around my shoulders and the four males growled. "Brayden, I—" I started, but he interrupted me.

"Jolie is my betrothed," Brayden informed them.

"Only if you pass the Gauntlet," I reminded him. "Not that I doubt you."

"Baby," the wolf whispered. "You're stronger than him."

"Come," I ordered the visitors. "Let's get you to your rooms."

Without waiting for anymore disruptions, I headed into the castle. The four followed me silently. Inside the hallway, guards watched us. I hadn't seen so many guards in the castle before, which meant Brayden had called them in. We walked to the visitor rooms, and I pushed open one of the doors and walked inside. All four entered without waiting for my invitation, the last one, the elf, closed the door.

I spun around and threw my arms around the nearest one. The five of us were connected, which made me believe they were the mates my bloodstones were connected to.

"I'm sorry," I whispered into his ear, feeling like an idiot for just throwing my arms around him, but it was my body's desire to touch them.

"You don't recognize us," he realized and hugged me tightly. It was the wolf.

"I do and I don't. I am pretty certain that you are my mates and we're connected, but I can't remember your names or anything about you. I suspected Brayden was lying to me, but I don't remember anything other than living here and him being betrothed to me since we were born."

"You locked down our bonds, so he couldn't get to us," the mage said.

"What?" I asked. "I don't know what you're talking about."

"This is incredibly powerful magic," the mage whispered.

"How do we break it?" the dragon asked.

"You could try kissing me," I suggested and smirked up at the wolf holding me.

He didn't hesitate. He pressed his lips to mine and with a hand on my upper back and one on my lower back, pulled me against him as tightly as he could.

When we separated, I smirked and said, "Well, it didn't work, but at least it was enjoyable."

"Baby," he whispered and touched my lower lip with his thumb. "We told you to stay safe."

"I'm alive," I said. "I'm still here…somewhere. I hope."

"I can break it," the mage said. "But, he'll know immediately that it's broken."

I stepped back and shook my head. "Not yet. I need you to win the Gauntlet first."

"So, you and he didn't…" the elf asked and trailed off.

I shook my head. "He may control me to a certain extent, but I am still me. I know I'm not his. I know I have mates." I tapped the bloodstones under my eye. "I know I belong to others. Plus, it is against the law to have sexual relations before they win the Gauntlet."

"At least there's that," the elf sighed.

"It's hard to explain. It's like he took segments of my memory and locked them up, so I can't access them. I get feelings, like about you four, but I don't know your names or what happened to me."

"Where's your friend? The one teaching you about being an empath?" the mage asked.

"Who?"

He scowled.

"You were with two friends," the dragon told me. "People you knew from your childhood."

My brows furrowed, and I tried to get the memory to surface, but it wouldn't. My head began to throb, and I clutched at it.

"That's enough," the mage said and pulled me against his chest with a hand to the back of my head. "Don't try to think any harder or you'll hurt yourself."

"I'm sorry," I whispered and felt tears stinging my eyes. "I wish I could break this now, but I need to be sure I can get rid of him when I do. He needs to pay for what he's done. Even if I can't remember exactly what he has done right now."

"We know what he's done," the wolf said with a snarl. "We'll make sure he pays."

I believed him. Looking at the four males before me, I believed they could win the Gauntlet and defeat Brayden.

Someone knocked on the door and the guys quickly moved so that I was hidden behind them.

"Enter," the dragon called.

"Is she—"

The door was shut and they moved aside so I could see a guard.

"He's a guard—" I started, but he rushed forward and hugged me.

"Jo," he whispered. "Jo, you're alive."

"Sort of," I mumbled as I inhaled his familiar scent. Who was he?

"She doesn't know who you are," the dragon told him.

The man released me and jerked backward. "No. He got you?"

"Brayden? Yeah."

He snarled and ran a hand through his hair. "Dammit. I knew I shouldn't have left you alone. What about Colton or Leona? I couldn't find them and—"

My head felt like it had cracked as images of the two sirens he was talking about slipped through the barrier Brayden had put up. I yelped and fell, but four pairs of arms caught me at the same time, cradling me between them all.

"Dungeons," I gasped out. "They're both in the dungeons."

"You cracked the spell a bit," the mage told him. "Crap."

"I have to go," I gasped and pushed away, tears in my eyes again.

"We'll win the Gauntlet," the elf promised me. "We'll free you from his spell."

I nodded and dashed outside, running down the hall and into Brayden. I cried and hugged him. "There you are! I was so scared! I thought you were gone."

"Why would I be gone?" he asked, petting my hair.

"I heard a guard say you were gone. I must have misheard him," I lied and looked up at him, batting his eyelashes. "Are you done at the arena? Can we have dinner together?"

He smiled wide and ran the back of his hand down my cheek. "I'm done with work. Let's go get some dinner."

I nodded and let him escort me, arm in arm, to the dining hall.

CHAPTER 9

Brayden kept close to me, meeting me for every meal and insisting that I accompany him to the meetings he held with the Elders. I knew he was keeping me from seeing the four males, my mates, but I did not call him on it. The Gauntlet wasn't too far away, and I couldn't risk Brayden finding out that his magic wasn't working one hundred percent on me.

Dad stayed holed up in his chambers, refusing to see me. I tried not to let it bother me, but I was getting really worried about him. Why wouldn't he want to see me? I was his daughter, his heir. He went so far as to order me to stay out of the wing of the castle his chambers were in.

I suspected Brayden had a hand in Dad's actions, but I did not have any proof.

Brayden and I walked in the garden and I saw the four males on the far side, their bodies glistening in the sun with sweat from working out. I was sad that I hadn't been able to see them practicing but knew I couldn't voice that opinion.

They headed in our direction, putting shirts on, which made me want to pout even more. Brayden draped his arm over my shoulders and pulled me against his side. If I acted different, he would know I wasn't completely under his control, so I played along, sidling up closer and smiled up at him.

"How can I help you gentlemen?" Brayden asked them.

All four were glaring at him. The wolf's eyes were glued to his arm around me.

"We were hoping to talk to the princess," the dragon said.

"Me?" I asked. "What about?"

"We wanted to talk to you in private," the dragon said.

"She will not be left alone with four outsiders," Brayden said. "You could kill her."

"We won't kill her, and you know that," the mage said with a scowl.

"I'm her guard, so if you want to talk to her, you have to talk to her with me present," Brayden told them with a smug smirk.

"What if I met with them in my office?" I asked Brayden. "You could stand guard outside my door to ensure they didn't try anything."

"No," Brayden said and glared down at me. "I will not allow you to be with them, alone."

I returned his glare and said, "You know I don't like being ordered around."

His gaze softened, and he smiled and put a hand on my cheek. "Sorry, sweetheart. I just want to make sure you are safe. If you were injured, or killed, I would be devastated."

"I don't think they have any ill will towards me," I said and looked at the males once before looking back at Brayden. "It's a normal protocol for the heir to meet with royals of other areas. They're princes, right? I should have met with them individually when they arrived."

"No," Brayden said again.

I pushed away from him and put my hands on my hips. "You can't change protocol."

"You can't put yourself in danger. We are so close to the Gauntlet and to our mating," Brayden whispered.

"They are also participating for my hand," I reminded him. "It's better for us if we show them proper courtesies."

"Come," Brayden said and grabbed my hand.

The four males moved a step forward, their eyes glowing.

Brayden's trident appeared in his hand and he aimed it at them.

I stepped between them and raised my hands. "Whoa. Stop. No fighting."

"We apologize," the elf said, and the four males backed up two steps, though their eyes didn't stop glowing.

Brayden's trident disappeared, and he put his hand on the small of my back and pushed me away from them. "Have a good night, gentlemen."

He hurried me along, and I barely had a chance to turn and look back at them. They looked furious and sad at the same time. My heart ached seeing them like that, knowing that I was the cause of it.

"You should be more respectful of the visiting royals," I told Brayden. "There was nothing wrong with them asking for a meeting with me."

"You are still too naïve," Brayden snapped. "Those males are dangerous. They are powerful and together, they might be able to overpower you."

"I'm not defenseless," I reminded him.

He smirked. "I know."

We walked into the castle and towards my room.

I paused in front of my door and turned to face him with a serious scowl. "The next time you order me around in front of other royals, I will have to punish you. You are not prince. You do not have power over me."

He opened his mouth to protest, but I held my hand up.

"I don't care that you're my guard. No one tells my dad what to do and you won't tell me what to do either. Are we clear? If you can't follow those simple rules, I will find a new guard."

Brayden's eyes hardened, and my head began to throb. "No. That won't do at all. I can't have you being so strong willed against me."

The pain intensified, and I dropped to my knees. "What are you doing?" I gasped.

He set his fingers on my temples and I began to black out. "Making you a bit more compliant. We've still got a week left until the Gauntlet and I don't want those assholes ruining my plans. I've worked too hard for too long to have them waltz in here and ruin it all."

The pain became so unbearable that I fainted.

"Princess Jolie," the dragon prince said and bowed to me as I walked by him.

"Good afternoon, Prince," I replied in greeting and dipped my head.

"Can I help you?" Brayden asked him.

The dragon smiled. "No, I was just out for a walk around your castle and wanted to say hello to the gorgeous princess as we passed each other."

I blushed. He thought I was gorgeous?

"You've said your greeting, now excuse us. We have things to do," Brayden said.

I glanced at the dragon prince as we walked away, and he winked at me. Before Brayden noticed, I turned back around. We continued down the hallway towards the dining hall.

Brayden pushed open the doors but froze when we found the mage prince and the werewolf prince sitting at one of the tables. They stood when we entered and bowed to me.

"You aren't supposed to bow to others of similar stature," I chastised them.

"We will always bow to you," the wolf said and smiled sweetly.

"What? Why?" I asked, unsure what he meant by that.

The mage pulled out a chair and smiled warmly. "Would you like to eat with us?"

I moved a step forward, but Brayden put his arm out. "No," he answered.

"Brayden, what's wrong?" I asked, looking at the two princes and then at him. He acted like they were a danger, but they didn't seem like they might be aggressive towards me.

"I don't trust them," he told me.

"We won't hurt her," the wolf said with a smile that wasn't exactly reassuring.

"It's just a meal," the mage said and tilted his head as he looked at Brayden. "Surely you can't think us sharing a meal with the princess is a problem? We weren't suggesting you leave. We understand, as her guard, that you would be standing at her back the entire time."

"Why don't you have guards?" I asked.

"We have no use for guards," the wolf said. "They would just slow us down."

"Please," the mage said. "Join us for a meal."

"It's only proper courtesy," I whispered to Brayden. "Please stop making a scene."

He was silent a moment and then he relented and pulled a chair out for me, one several away from the princes. I sat and smiled happily.

The mage took his seat beside the wolf and they smiled at me.

"So, Princess, what do you do for fun here?" the wolf asked.

"I like to go for walks and read," I answered.

"You don't play games?" the mage asked.

My head throbbed a moment, but it quickly passed.

Weird.

"No," Brayden said. "We don't."

"Sounds pretty boring," the wolf commented.

"Books are rarely boring," I told him.

"Do you have a library?" the mage asked.

I nodded and smiled wide. "Yes! It's quite large."

He smiled back. "I'd love to see it. Perhaps after we eat, you could show me?"

"I would love—"

"Your meal, Princess," Brayden said, interrupting me.

A servant set plates in front of me and the two princes, then set two more in front of the two empty chairs across from me.

The dragon and elf princes walked in and took the empty seats, smiling at me.

"Hello, princes," I said in greeting to them.

"Hello, Princess," the elf said. "You look lovely, as always."

Heat spread along my cheeks. "Thank you."

"Eat," Brayden said. "I have errands to attend to."

"You could just go on your errands while I eat," I said and put my napkin on my lap.

"We'd be happy to keep the princess company," the wolf said with a wink at me.

Be still my heart! I might melt into a puddle of goo in my chair if the four sexy males didn't stop flirting with me.

"Out of the question," Brayden said.

"Why not ask one of the other guards to guard me while you go on your errands?" I asked him.

"No. That's final," Brayden snapped.

I frowned at him. "Okay. You don't have to snap at me."

"Such rudeness aimed at your princess is uncalled for," the elf said and tsked his tongue. "I can't remember the last time I heard of a guard acting like that with a royal."

"We've known each other since we were born and he's my betrothed," I said. "Sometimes he forgets the boundaries guards are supposed to follow."

Brayden said nothing, but I knew he was probably mad.

"I'll eat fast," I said and glanced at him with a smile. "Then we can go on your errands."

"Thank you," he said and relaxed slightly.

The princes didn't seem to like my response.

We ate and they kept casting weird glances at me. What were they thinking? What was going on with them?

"Thank you for joining me for a meal," I said as I finished and stood.

The four stood and then bowed to me.

Why were they bowing? They shouldn't have been bowing to me.

"I hope you have an enjoyable night," the elf said.

"You as well," I said and smiled at him. He smiled and it lit up his entire face.

Damn, they were so handsome.

"Come," Brayden said and nudged me forward.

I obeyed, heading out of the dining hall despite the strange desire to stay and not only talk to the four princes, but touch them. I hadn't even kissed Brayden, so why was I having these strange desires with these males I barely knew?

"You shouldn't trust others so easily," Brayden chastised me.

"I wasn't trusting them, really. It is proper for me to meet with them. I'm not sure why you trust them so little. They don't seem like they hold any aggression towards me. If anyone, it seems like they hate you."

He scowled. "I don't care what they think about me."

"You've been acting strange lately," I whispered. "What's wrong? Are you worried that you won't win the Gauntlet? Or are you worried that you might have to share me with another male?"

He stopped and turned to look at me. "What do you mean share you?"

"Well, it is written in the laws that the winners of the Gauntlet get to claim my hand. Winners as in plural. So, if you and one or two of the others win, then I would be mated to all of you," I explained.

"Where did you read that?" he asked, his brows furrowing and fists clenching at his side.

Why was he mad? That was the way our laws were written hundreds of years ago.

"It is written that way in the laws," I said. "The original laws from our inception here in Atlantis."

"We'll see about that," he snapped and resumed walking.

"You can't change the laws," I said and hurried to catch up to him.

He stopped again and faced me. "Do you want one of those other males as your mate?"

"I didn't say that," I said and hoped I wasn't blushing again.

"We have been betrothed since birth. Why would you want to change that now?" he asked, sounding hurt.

"I don't want to change it, but the laws are the laws and we must follow them."

"Sometimes laws are meant to be changed. Sometimes laws become outdated and need a refresher," he countered.

"You don't just go change the laws when they don't suit you," I said with a scoff. "Besides, they may all fail in the very first round for all we know. Stop worrying so much about the laws. You should be focusing on training and ensuring you're prepared for the Gauntlet."

"Don't worry about me," he said and smiled. "I've been preparing for this day my entire life. I will win the Gauntlet and I will make you my mate."

For the first time, I didn't like the idea of being his mate. There was something dark and sinister lurking beneath his cool exterior. What would happen if he lost?

His gaze softened, and he hugged me. "I'm sorry. I am very stressed out about the Gauntlet and I don't like having outsiders in Atlantis. It sets me on edge."

"They've done nothing that might be portrayed as indecent,

hostile, or marked them as suspicious," I said. "Why are you acting so hostile towards them?"

"You don't see it," he said. "They're up to something. They are plotting something."

His eyes were glowing with anger and I was fairly certain that he was the one plotting something. What? I had no idea, and that frightened me.

❀

As the sun set, I had Brayden take me to my chambers, feigning tiredness.

At my door, he hesitated, his brows pinched in worry. "Are you sure you don't want me to get a healer?" he asked.

I patted his cheek and smiled. "I'm sure it's just the nerves from the upcoming events. I am going to lie down and read a book until I fall asleep."

"Do you want me to stay with you?" he asked.

Tamping down the spike of fear, I smiled wider. "Always trying to break the rules, naughty boy. No, I'm sure you have things to take care of. Just post a soldier outside my door if it will help ease your worry. I won't leave my chambers."

He nodded and brushed his thumb over my cheek before barking orders at nearby guards and leaving.

I released a breath in relief and quickly locked my door behind me. It wouldn't do to have Brayden or the guards barge in. Especially, since I wouldn't be in my room.

Tapping on the walls lightly, it took me a couple minutes to locate the switch. The wall opened, and I stepped through, standing in a narrow passageway that wove all around the castle. Only Dad and I knew about these secret passages, this secret was only for the royal family. Dad said it was a safety precaution in case even the guards turned against the royal family. I was immensely grateful for it now.

I shut the opening to my room and followed the path, which was just wide enough for me to walk. I bet the elf prince's shoulders would get stuck if he tried to walk here.

There was something about those princes, something that drew me to them. I needed to talk to them, to find out what it was.

I paused at the piece of the wall that would open to the elf prince's room. He seemed the kindest of them all. I just hoped I wasn't wrong about them. I hoped I wasn't walking in to a death trap.

I strained to listen, to see if he was in his room.

"I'm telling you," the elf said, "I can feel her. She's close."

"He's right," the mage prince said. "But, I can't just teleport to her. She's probably with Trident Douche."

Trident Douche? It only took moments to realize they meant Brayden.

A giggle escaped before I slapped my hand over my mouth.

"What was that? That sounded like Jolie," the dragon said.

I pushed the lever and the wall split open. I smiled at the four princes who stood in varying stances.

The dragon prince moved towards me, but I backed up, my eyes widening. He froze.

"Wait," I pleaded. "I just wanted to talk."

The elf peered behind me. "Where's your guard?"

I shrugged. "He thinks I'm sleeping."

The mage waved me in. "Come in and I'll put a spell up so no one can hear us."

I nodded and stepped into the room, activating the switch so the door closed over the passageway. Inhaling, I drew in their four distinct scents and shuddered. They smelled familiar and good...no, great.

"Jolie," the wolf prince whispered and lifted his hand towards me, like he was going to touch my face, but then lowered it with a pained expression.

His pain was palpable. I wanted to touch him, to ease his pain, but I couldn't.

"First name basis?" I asked with a cheeky smirk. "I didn't realize we were so close already."

"Fuck, she's even worse than when we arrived," the dragon said, and his hands curled into fists at his sides.

"Jolie," the elf said softly. I turned to face him. "Do you remember us?" he asked.

I scowled. "You're the Four Princes of Jinla. Here to participate in the Gauntlet for a chance to become my mate."

"We are already your mates," the wolf said.

I rolled my eyes. "I think I'd remember having mates."

Especially ones as hot as you.

"Why can't we just kill him now?" the dragon asked, his eyes glowing angrily.

I took a step back, my mouth opening in surprise. "Kill? Who are you planning to kill?"

He held his hands up in surrender. "No one. I'm sorry. I'm just upset because you don't remember us."

"You really think we are already mates?" I asked and all four nodded. "If that's true, why don't I remember you or have a bond?"

"Your guard isn't what he seems," the wolf growled. "He's manipulating your memories."

I shook my head and backed up another step. "No, Brayden would never do something like that to me. He's my best friend."

Their jaws tensed and they all averted their eyes from mine.

"Prove to me what you're saying is true," I ordered them.

"We—" the mage began.

"Prove it or I will have you sent away and you'll lose your chance to participate in the Gauntlet," I threatened them.

The mage walked up to me and turned me so I faced the mirror on the wall. He pointed at my cheek. "If you're not mated, why do you have bloodstones?"

119

"There's nothing there," I told him. "You don't have bloodstones either."

His hands sparkled a moment, then it disappeared so quickly I thought I had imagined it.

"Nico, how is that possible?" the wolf asked. "How can he make her sight different?"

"I don't know," Nico growled and stomped away from me.

The elf touched my cheek, his fingertips warm. "You have two bloodstones right here," he said. He took my hand and pressed my fingertips to the same spot. For the briefest of moments, I felt the hard edges of the bloodstones, but then it was gone.

I shook my head. "I'm sorry. I—"

The elf hugged me and stroked my hair. "Don't worry. We will figure out a plan."

I melted against him, his body warm and his embrace...loving.

Another body wrapped around me from behind and without looking, I knew it was the wolf.

Every instinct told me to stay, but my brain forced me to jump away from them.

"No," I whispered, my body shaking with need to touch them. "I don't know you. You can't hold me or touch me in such a manner."

"Does it feel like you don't know us?" the dragon asked. He reached out slowly, giving me time to pull away, but I stayed still. He set his hand against my cheek and I leaned into it. "We are all connected," he whispered, then bent and brushed a feather light kiss across my lips.

Desire speared through me. My hands wrapped around the base of his neck and pulled him closer. He wrapped his arms around me and kissed me again, this time hard and fierce, his tongue sweeping across mine.

He tasted like...home.

I jerked away and held a hand out, warding him off. "No! No.

We aren't supposed to do anything like that until you win the Gauntlet." Backing up, I hit the lever and the wall opened.

"Don't go," the wolf begged, his eyes pleading and filled with sorrow.

"I'm sorry," I gasped, hot tears splashing down my cheeks. I stepped back into the passageway and hit the button, closing the wall before they could get to me. I ran, my hand over my mouth to hold in the sobs. Once back in my room, with the wall closed tight, I collapsed on my bed and cried.

Kissing the dragon had felt right, familiar. It didn't feel like it was my first kiss, but my hundredth with him.

Were they right? Were they my mates? Or was this some type of ploy to trick me into trusting them?

They hadn't seemed to be acting. Their reactions had been too real, too pained to be faked.

If that was true, what did that mean? Was someone else manipulating me?

They said it was Brayden, but I refused to believe that.

I shook my head back and forth hard.

No, it couldn't be Brayden. He would never do something like that to me.

Would he?

He had been acting strange and had been so adamant about me not spending time with the four princes. Was he trying to keep us apart so I wouldn't discover that I was connected to them?

After changing into pajamas, I lay beneath my covers and touched my lips. The kiss had definitely been enjoyable.

Brayden stopped by later that night, but I ignored his knocking. The door unlocked, and I tensed. Since when did he have a key to my room?

He bent over me and kissed my cheek. "Sleep well, Jolie. Soon, we will be mates. And, those princes will be gone for good."

Gone?

Brayden pulled my blanket up higher and I snuggled down into them, keeping my eyes closed, feigning sleep. He stayed a bit longer, then finally left. He was going to hurt them. I had to stop him.

❦

AT LUNCH, THE PRINCES JOINED BRAYDEN AND I AGAIN. THEY didn't act any different than they had been, thankfully, so Brayden was still left in the dark.

"Any plans today?" I asked Brayden as I ate a piece of fruit.

"I have some business with the Elders to attend to," he said.

"Would it be alright if I stayed behind?" I asked. "It's *so* boring."

He eyed the princes, but they were all very interested in their food at the moment.

"Very well. You may stay, but I need you to stay in your room with guards outside your doors and you not to let anyone inside. Understood?" Brayden said.

"Awfully pushy for a guard to his princess," one of them muttered, but I couldn't tell which one.

"I understand and agree," I said to Brayden, acting like I hadn't heard the prince. "Thank you. I want to finish that book I started yesterday."

"Are you finished eating?" he asked.

I nodded.

"I will escort you to your room then," he said and held out his hand.

I let him help me stand out of my chair, then slid my arm through his with a smile I hoped was warm. "Always the gentleman," I said and tugged him towards the door. "Let's go, so you can get to your meeting. I know you'll be there for hours, since any meeting with the Elders takes at least three."

Brayden sighed. "I fear this one might take four or five."

"Anything I should know?" I asked him, stepping out of the room and into the hallway without looking back at the princes, despite the burning urge to do so.

"No, it's nothing important. They just like to discuss things for hours at a time, no matter how trivial," Brayden said.

Brayden stationed two guards outside my room and waited until I closed and locked my door before leaving.

I waited five more minutes before slipping out of my room and into the secret passageway. My nerves were fried by the time I reached the elf prince's room, my hands shaking slightly.

"Rhys, calm down," the elf said. "It's hard for all of us to see her touch him."

"It's all an act," the wolf said. "Didn't you see her flinch when touching him?"

"It was super subtle, but she did," the mage said.

I knocked twice on the wall, then activated the switch and smiled at them. The dragon was looking out the patio doors and the other three sat around a table in the center of the room. Things were thrown around, like someone had a tantrum.

"Hi," I said nervously.

"We weren't sure you'd show," the mage said.

After closing the secret door, I faced them and said, "I don't believe you yet, about us being mates, but you're in danger. I don't know what he is planning, but Brayden intends to hurt or kill you."

The elf pulled out a chair at the table and waved me forward. I sat, and he kissed my cheek before taking his own seat.

"We know," the dragon said, still looking out the doors. "We are prepared for his attack."

"I want to stop him, but I don't know how. He keeps hiding me away from the others and won't even let me talk to the Elders without him. There's no reason for that, except if he is hiding things from me."

"We appreciate you wanting to help, but we want you to just

stay safe," the elf said. "We wouldn't have let you come here like this, except it's taking a toll on us not to have physical contact with you."

Their eyes were bloodshot, which was abnormal for Others.

I stood, walked to the elf, and slowly set my hand on his cheek.

His eyelids fluttered closed and he exhaled a shaky breath. I reached over with my other hand to touch the mage's neck, since he was the next closest.

He set his hand atop mine and sighed with a smile on his face, then closed his eyes.

"Come on," I coaxed the wolf and dragon who were staring at me. "I only have two hands, but you can come touch me. In appropriate places."

They didn't hesitate, both walking to me and putting a hand on each of my arms.

Joy and love surrounded my heart and I felt our connection.

"We really are mates," I whispered in shock. How were the bonds blocked? Why would Brayden do that? Why would he make me forget my mates?

"Yes, my love. We are," the wolf whispered in my ear.

I leaned back against the wolf and dragon and let their love surround and fill me. We had to stop Brayden. No matter what.

"You should return to your room," the dragon whispered against my hair.

"Five more minutes," I whispered back.

The elf pressed his hand over mine on his cheek and with all four touching my skin, I felt happy and content for the first time in weeks.

What was I going to do?

"I don't want you to leave," the mage whispered, "but we can't risk him finding out you know. The last two times you broke part of his spell, he made it worse, to the point that you didn't even know us."

"What?" I asked in disbelief.

"It's too much to explain right now," the mage said. "Just, trust us. We're working on a plan and we know that he is likely to attack us or send people after us. We aren't weak and we work together, so none of us will be caught unaware or alone." He stood from his chair and the others retreated a step back, so only the mage was touching me or in my line of sight. "Please, Jolie, stay safe. We can protect you, but not while you're with him, away from us. Would you consider letting me stay in your room with you?"

"He'll see you when he comes in the morning," I said, swallowing roughly.

"I can use an invisibility spell," the mage explained.

I shook my head and chewed on my lip. "I didn't want to tell you, but…he has a key to my room. I don't know when he had one made or how he got it, but last night when I didn't answer him because I was pretending to sleep, he unlocked my door and came in."

All of them tensed. I felt the tension in the room like a blanket pulled over my head.

"Did he touch you?" the dragon asked quietly.

I didn't like the way he spoke. I didn't like this quiet side of him. "No. He kissed my forehead, but he didn't touch me inappropriately."

"If he tries, or if you feel that you're in danger with him, scream and I'll come," the mage said.

"We'll all come with him," the wolf promised. "If you're in trouble, the four of us will come protect you."

"I wish the Gauntlet was here already, so we could just get this shit over with," I grumbled and leaned my forehead against the mage's chest.

He slid his fingers into my hair and gripped the back of my head. "Me too, love. Me too."

The other three joined us again, all touching me where they could, and we stood like that for another couple of minutes.

"I need to get back," I whispered.

"Do you want me to teleport you back?" the mage asked.

"Okay," I agreed.

"Wait," the wolf said. He leaned forward and kissed me lightly on the lips. "Goodnight, Jolie."

"Night," I whispered.

The elf and dragon gave me kisses as well, all of them feather light and sweet. It drove me crazy.

The mage linked our fingers together and then teleported us into my room. I tensed, waiting for Brayden to jump out and catch us, but he didn't. Everything was quiet.

"Thank you," I whispered to the mage. "Thank you for caring for me."

He kissed me and leaned his forehead against mine, our noses barely touching and whispered, "I love you, more than anything else in the world. I lost you once and I won't lose you again. Stay safe, my queen." He kissed me again, then disappeared.

What did he mean that he had lost me once?

I ate dinner alone, mulling over everything, then sat in silence in my room until I was exhausted and ready to sleep.

I went to bed and my dreams were filled with the princes, my mates, and when I woke, I knew they were not dreams, but memories.

CHAPTER 10

"Welcome!" the announcer yelled. "This is the first Gauntlet in over thirty years!"

The crowd cheered, and I shifted nervously on my throne. Dad sat beside me on his throne, a huge smile on his face.

The arena was located on the outskirts of Atlantis and rose more than two hundred feet high on the outside. The inner walls were over eighty feet high. It was oval shaped, with a raised platform on the southern side. Dad and my thrones sat on the raised platform, giving us the ability to see the entire arena easily. Plus, it separated us from the citizens.

The attendee seats were filled, which wasn't surprising since not much happened in Atlantis. This was the most interesting thing to happen in decades.

The four outsiders stood in the center of the arena, side by side, with Brayden a bit away from them. Brayden had his trident in one hand, the base resting on the sandy arena floor.

"Who do you think will win?" Dad asked.

"The four newcomers," I answered honestly.

Dad looked over at me. "Them? You don't think Brayden will win?"

"I hope not," I whispered.

Dad's eyes widened, but I put my finger to my lips and shook my head. This was not the place to discuss this.

"The first event is a race," the announcer said. "The race will begin here, go to the fountain in Shelnam, and then return to the stadium." The announcer showed the participants and attendees a bird's eye view of the path.

The mage raised his hand and asked, "Is magic permitted?"

"I'm getting there," the announcer grumbled. "The rules for the race are as follows: no killing and no involving anyone not part of the race."

The mage smiled and cracked his knuckles.

My other three mates stretched and jogged in place to warm up. Brayden's trident shrank down to pen size and he put it in his pocket.

Well, now we knew where he kept it. I never knew it shrank like that.

"Get ready," the announcer called.

The wolf shifted into his warrior form and stood ready at the line. The dragon let wings out of his back and stood between the wolf and mage. The elf's body glowed when he took his place.

Brayden's eyes widened as he looked at them, and I saw worry for the first time. He hadn't been able to compare himself to anyone aside from other Atlantis inhabitants. He had no idea what these four princes were capable of.

"On your marks!"

They all stood at attention, except the mage who was examining his fingernails.

"Get set!"

Their bodies tensed. The entire arena was silent as the audience sat in rapt attention.

"Go!"

A horn blew and all took off without the mage. He looked up at me, winked, then snapped his fingers. One moment he was in the arena, the next he was at the fountain in Shelnam, then with one more snap, he stood back in the arena, just a step before the finish line.

Teleportation!

I tore my eyes away from him to find Brayden just making it to Shelnam, a rather impressive time by Atlantis comparisons. The others, however, were already running back into the arena. He was no match for them in speed, it seemed. The four friends crossed the finish line side by side, so that they were all first place and Brayden came in last. Brayden panted and a scowled at the four smiling princes.

"The four princes win with a tie," the announcer said, disbelief coloring his tone.

I restrained from cheering, despite the urge to do so.

"Next is a battle," the announcer said, coming back to his usual character. "Weapons and magic are permitted. No killing. If you kill your opponent, you're disqualified. Winner will be by knockout, yield, or incapacitation. I have the right to stop the battle if I think the person is incapable of protecting themselves."

Brayden pulled out his trident and the crowd cheered. The elf and wolf drew swords from seemingly thin air, while the dragon shifted into warrior form, and the mage made a staff appear from the center of one palm.

"Ready?" the announcer asked.

The five males raised their arms in acknowledgement.

"Begin!"

Brayden raised his trident and pointed it at the four standing across from him. They didn't move. He smiled victoriously and walked towards them with his trident still raised.

"It appears Brayden has frozen them!" the announcer yelled as the crowd cheered loudly.

Brayden moved closer and still the four didn't move.

"No," I whispered. This couldn't be it. They couldn't lose so easily!

The mage tilted his head to look at me and he smiled.

Brayden moved to stab the mage, who was still looking at me, but his trident hit an invisible wall.

The mage turned to face Brayden and said, "You caught me off guard with that once. I'm not stupid enough to fall for it again."

The wolf and dragon raced forward together, attacking Brayden simultaneously. They moved around each other with no sounds and yet never bumped into each other. They ducked when one swung, or jumped when needed, with no verbal communication. Had they known each other a long time and just knew how the other fought? Or did they have some type of mental communication?

Brayden tried to freeze them with his trident's power, but the mage was protecting them. He fought back, but he couldn't defeat two of them. His eyes flicked to me and suddenly my legs were moving, carrying me away from the throne I had been sitting on. I walked to the edge of the raised platform, over two hundred feet above the arena floor.

The elf looked up and his eyes widened when he saw me. "Rhys, switch!" he yelled.

The dragon, Rhys, spun and raced back, while the elf ran past him to attack Brayden.

I stepped forward and fell.

People screamed.

I screamed.

Rhys leapt into the sky with newly sprouted wings and caught me. "I got you, baby."

I clutched him and gasped for air. "He…he tried to kill me!"

"He knew we'd be distracted and want to protect you," Rhys said and set me back before my throne. "He just didn't know it wouldn't help him."

I sat down and Dad reached over to squeeze my arm.

Rhys bowed to me and flew back down to the fight, his entire body rigid with anger. He landed behind Brayden and shifted into a huge dragon. He roared, and fire spewed from his mouth, covering the entire arena, including his friends.

People screamed again.

Had he killed the other three? Had he murdered his friends just to kill Brayden?

The fire disappeared, and my three mates stood, unscathed, bathed in a silver light. The mage must have protected them.

Brayden lay on the ground, water surrounding him in a protective spell all sirens knew. The left side of his face was burnt as were his clothes.

Rhys reverted back to his human form and said, "Next time you try to hurt my mate, I'll swallow you whole."

The water evaporated in a wisp and Brayden moaned.

The announcer raced down to Brayden and checked his vitals. "He's alive, but unable to continue. He loses and the Four Princes of Jinla win."

Some in the crowd cheered, but most stared in disbelief.

"Your Highness," Sam said and knelt before me.

"Did you do as I asked?"

He nodded. "Yes, Your Highness."

Aside from memories of my mates, I had a few memories of my childhood return last night as well. Among them were my best friends: Sam, Leona, and Colton.

"Announcer!" I called.

He looked up at me, stepping to the side as healers came out to tend to Brayden.

"The quest is ready," I informed him.

His eyes widened, and he looked at Brayden's unconscious form. "But he—"

"He is unfit to continue," I said. "Or do you think I should lower myself to accept subpar mates?"

131

He stuttered and sputtered a moment before composing himself. "Very well, let's move to the third event, the quest."

"Quest?" Rhys asked.

I walked to the edge of the platform and addressed everyone. "Something precious to me has been hidden in Atlantis. You have twelve hours to find and bring this precious thing to me."

"Do we get any clues?" the mage asked.

"It's from my childhood here in Atlantis. And, it's something I would die for." I said, praying it was enough of a clue for them to figure it out.

"Wait!" Brayden snarled, limping towards the center of the arena. "I'm participating too."

"Very well," I agreed without hesitation. "Your time begins now."

Brayden hobbled back out.

Rhys took to the sky in his dragon form. The elf ran from the arena. The mage teleported out, but I had no idea where he went to. The wolf looked up at me for a long moment, then a huge smile split his face and he turned into a wolf before running out of the arena.

"Shall we get some food while we wait?" Dad asked.

"I can't leave the arena," I reminded him.

"Sam, have another guard fetch us food," Dad said.

Sam nodded and went to the nearest guard to order him to do so.

Pillows were brought out and I gratefully accepted two, putting them on my throne and sighing at the relief on my butt. "Much better."

Dad chuckled. "We should put some padding on these thrones."

"It would make them much more comfortable."

"I'll have someone work on that after the Gauntlet," Dad promised.

"Sounds great," I said. I didn't want to point out that I

wouldn't be here long. Once we defeated Brayden, I was out of here. I had no desire to rule Atlantis.

"Here you go, Your Majesty," one guard said as he and three other guards set up a buffet of food on a table before us.

I filled up my plate and ate it quickly, filling my plate up for a second and then third time before I was full.

"Quite the appetite," Sam commented.

"Shut up," I ordered him and growled.

"Do you think any of them will be able to figure the quest out?" Dad asked.

"I hope so," I muttered. "If anyone can do it, I think the princes can."

"You have high hopes for those ones," Dad commented.

"Yes, I do," I agreed.

"Brayden isn't a bad person," Dad said. "He's strong and he is a siren."

"He's not just a siren. I don't know what else he is, but he's something else too," I whispered.

"Why do you think that?" Dad asked. "You haven't even been home for a month and you think you know him better than I do after over twenty years?"

"Yes," I said bluntly.

"The princess may be on to something," Sam whispered at my side.

Dad glanced at him, then focused back on me. "He is your betrothed," he reminded me.

"I was banished, so he should have stopped being my betrothed," I said. "Honestly, has my banishment even ended? Is the Gauntlet necessary since I'm still banished?"

Dad frowned as he thought about it. "I guess that's true. I never unbanished you."

"Don't!" I hissed. "If I stay banished, it might come in handy soon."

"How could being banished be handy?" Sam asked.

"You never know," I whispered.

I chewed on a bread roll as we continued to wait and I thought about the four males who had come. They were obviously friends and they worked flawlessly together. How did I fit into the equation? Did I fit flawlessly as well? What if my memory never came back? What if Brayden found a way to permanently break me?

They were my mates, that was obvious by the two blood-stones beneath my eye that carried blood from two of them in each one. It was interesting that they did two in one instead of four in one or just four individual stones. Perhaps I hadn't wanted to have four stones.

"Would you like some dessert?" Sam asked me.

I nodded emphatically. "Yes, please."

He nodded at the guard who had brought us back the food and the guard hurried off. It was nice having guards to do things for me. But, I would prefer not to have guards and to be free. Would I still be free if the princes were my mates? Would we have guards or servants? Where did we live? I had no idea where or what was going on when it came to them.

"With four mates, that greatly increases my chances of becoming a grandfather," Dad said. "It's hard for siren females to conceive, so four mates would definitely increase those odds."

"Could you not talk about my sex life?" I growled.

"Children are important. We need to continue the royal line," Dad said.

"Well, then why didn't you just remarry?" I asked.

"There is no one who can compare to your mother," he whispered, and a wistful expression crossed his face. "She was perfect."

"She was," Sam agreed.

"I wish I could remember her," I whispered. I wished I could remember a lot of things.

"She loved you," Dad whispered. "More than anything else in

the world. She would be proud to see you as you are. You're a lot like her. So proud and beautiful. She never backed down when she truly believed in something."

"Definitely sounds like our Jolie," Rhys said.

Sam, Dad, and I jumped at the sudden appearance of Rhys, the mage, the wolf, and the elf.

"What are you doing here?" I asked. "You haven't completed the quest yet, have you?"

Leona and Colton stepped from behind them and I flew into their arms. "You're okay!"

They hugged me back tightly.

"You're not," Leona whispered. "And it's all my fault."

"It's not your fault," I assured her.

"We need to defeat him. Now," Colton said.

"Dad, they won. They found what I'd hidden. You need to announce them as the winners," I said urgently.

Dad nodded, stood, and opened his mouth, but no sound came out.

"Not. So. Fast," Brayden hissed. He held a dagger to the back of my father and glared at us.

"You've lost," I told him. "You lost the Gauntlet and you've lost Atlantis. Just give up."

"No!" he snapped. "This is my kingdom and I will not let these scumbags ruin it for me!"

Sam moved back behind the thrones, his position hidden from Brayden.

"This is not your kingdom! Atlantis will never bow to you," I growled.

"You aren't even princess," Brayden said with a sneer. "You're still banished."

"Even if you win today, then what? You think I'm going to sit demurely by your side while you rule?"

"No, I'll kill you as soon as we're wed," he said.

My four mates growled and took a step closer, but Brayden

stuck the knife against my father's back, making my dad hiss in pain as it pierced the skin.

"Not a step closer," he ordered them.

"You're pathetic," I growled. "You can't even fight me yourself. You have to resort to using a hostage. How do you think you can rule Atlantis when a poor, defenseless girl like me frightens you?"

"You don't frighten me," he said and scoffed. I could smell the lie instantly.

"Fight me, then," I challenged him. "You win, and you get Atlantis. I win, and you die," I said.

He thought about it. "Your mates aren't allowed to interfere."

I rolled my eyes. "Obviously. I challenged you to a duel, not to fight all of us."

"Deal," he said and lowered the knife.

The idiot had no idea what he'd done. Rushing forward, I grabbed him by the front of his shirt and tossed him sideways, away from my father. The elf was nearest him and he attempted to stab him, but Brayden rolled out of the way.

The men began attacking him, four of them against just Brayden. Brayden did something to me that made me cry out in pain and clutch my head. Brayden's power cracked into the wall I had built around my bonds and surged down Rhys's bond.

"No!" I screamed.

Rhys froze, his eyes rolling up into his head a moment, then he began to attack the wolf.

"Nico!" the wolf yelled as he protected himself against Rhys.

The mage, Nico, cursed and ran to me. "It's now or never, love."

I tried to say something, but Brayden sent more power into my head and tried to get to Nico's bond.

Nico whispered a spell quickly beneath his breath and slowly, painfully, began to push Brayden out of my head.

"Just a bit more," he whispered as I screamed.

Slowly, the pain eased and when it did, I was alone in my head again. But, the memories were still locked away.

"You kill me and she'll never get her memory back!" Brayden hissed. He lay on the ground with the wolf holding him while the elf held a sword to his throat.

"I can't remember," I whispered and looked up at Nico. "I don't remember still."

"Unlock her memories now!" the mage bellowed, his body glowing as he struggled to control his fury. Sparks fizzled at his fingertips.

I giggled and they all looked at me. "Sparkles," I said and looked right at Nico. "You're Sparkles."

"Yes," he whispered and turned to me. "Do you remember?"

"She won't. I've locked them down too tightly," Brayden said smugly. "I reinforced them after Sam put a crack in it."

"We should just kill him," the wolf snarled.

"If you do, I'll never get my memories back," I said softly. I would never know what happened to me. Or who I was.

"We can make new memories," the elf said. "I would rather have you, without your memories, than risk him hurting you more."

"I don't even know your names," I said with tears in my eyes, momentarily blinding me. I hurriedly wiped them away.

"Nico," the wolf said, "I have an idea."

Rhys took the wolf's spot, holding Brayden down, so the wolf could walk to us. He whispered in Nico's ear, then looked at me with a smile.

Nico thought about it for several tense and silent moments, then nodded. "It might work." He stood before me and I shrank back at his intense stare. His gaze softened and he brushed my hair away from my face. "This might hurt, but I'll try to minimize that as much as possible."

The wolf stood beside Nico and me, a warm smile on his face. "Just try to relax, okay?"

I nodded. These males were not likely to try to hurt me. At least, not on purpose. They were my mates, whether I remembered fully or not.

Nico placed his fingers against my temples and closed his eyes. "Okay," he said.

The wolf set his fingers atop Nico's and took a steadying breath before closing his eyes.

I followed suit, closing my eyes, and waiting.

I saw myself standing on a bus, looking at a strange electronic device. I had always wanted to ride on a bus. The bus stopped, and as I reached for my bag, a male snatched it and ran off the bus. I heard myself yell, but then I saw the bag snatcher on the ground, under a foot.

"This was the day I met you," the wolf's voice whispered in my head.

An arm appeared, holding my bag out to me, as I walked to him. I looked happy, but there were heavy bags beneath my eyes and my body seemed frail.

I was seeing the wolf's memories!

The image changed to me sitting across from the wolf at a restaurant. The dress I had on was pretty and I chatted with him about something...a game of some sort.

More memories played, some were very intimate, and I felt my face flush since Nico was likely seeing them as well. Deryn. The wolf's name was Deryn.

"Sam, swap with Fox," Deryn ordered him.

The memories stopped, but Nico kept his fingers on my temples.

"You okay?" he asked.

I nodded.

"Any new memories?" he asked.

"No," I replied softly. "But, I think it's helping."

The elf walked over. he was the shortest of the four, but

extremely muscular. He was also the happiest of the bunch, radiating joy, even now.

"Ready, cupcake?" he asked.

"Yes."

He set his fingers on top of Nico's and we all closed our eyes.

The first memory was me, sitting in a park with crossed legs and closed eyes, grumbling to myself. It looked like I was trying to meditate. The elf sat beside me and we talked, then walked around the park together. Another memory showed me sitting on a sidewalk, looking scared and sad. The elf's body shrank down and he crawled into my lap. Another memory, me standing while Fox, that was his name, and the other three bowed to me. Four princes bowing to me.

The shell around my memories cracked more.

"No!" Brayden yelled.

"Rhys," Fox said. "Your turn."

Rhys took his place and funneled memories of fun, pleasure, and fighting. He was always fighting for me. Even with the bond closed, I could tell he loved me. It was evident in how he always kept an eye on me wherever we were and in how he would caress me while I slept.

They all loved me.

Rhys stepped back and wiped away a tear that had fallen from my eyes. "Did I hurt you?" he asked.

"You love me, so much," I whispered.

He smiled. "We do."

The shell cracked a little more, allowing a few memories to slip out. The memories weren't nice ones, but painful experiences of mine. A woman severing my bonds with the princes was the first, and the second was of me trapped in a cupboard of some sort.

I whimpered, and Nico began to funnel his memories to me.

"Yes, there are lots of painful memories."

He showed me a memory of me being stabbed at a party.

139

"But, there are also happy ones."

This memory was of a holiday event, all of us together and laughing, while eating desserts.

The shell broke apart and my memories rushed forward. Nico broke contact with me and gasped in pain as he fell to his knees.

New hands touched my head and slowed the memories, letting them funnel through at a pace that was not as painful. When the last memory was set in place, I opened my eyes to find Leona holding me.

"Leona," I whispered, my voice hoarse as though I'd been yelling.

"I owed you," she said softly.

"Did-did you see them?"

She nodded. "I'm so sorry that you endured so much."

"You've ruined everything!" Brayden screamed.

Everyone froze. Nico was weak from helping me and couldn't counter him.

Brayden shoved Sam and Fox away and stood. "This isn't over," Brayden snarled at me.

Leona's hands dropped, and I was able to move. I faced Brayden and sang the lullaby my grandmother had taught me. At the time, I thought it was just a lullaby, but now I knew. It was a siren's call, but one for empaths to use against sirens. It enraptured them.

Brayden jerked back, his eyes wide. I continued to sing, power pouring from me in waves. His legs trembled and he screamed. He stabbed his trident in its small, pen-sized form into his leg, breaking my hold and fled.

I collapsed to the stone floor of the platform and smiled. He may have escaped, but I was back to my old self.

CHAPTER 11

Brayden had escaped Atlantis, but that was no longer important.

Dad stood before me, scowling as he looked at me and my four mates. "You are princess here," he said.

"Technically, I'm still banished. Plus, I have my hands full back in Jinla," I said.

"I don't think she could survive a month without her video games," Nico whispered.

The other three chuckled in agreement.

I would have argued, but he was right.

"You can make someone else your heir," I said.

"Any suggestions?" he asked me and sat on his throne.

"Sam," I said without hesitation. "He is one hundred percent loyal to the royal family. And, he's a decent fighter."

Dad tapped the arm of his throne, a solid gold and jewel covered monstrosity, as he thought about it. "Very well."

"I'd like to leave tomorrow morning," I told him.

He sighed and his eyes dropped to the floor at my feet. "Okay."

if it's alright with you, I'd like to come visit from time to time. I know I'm banished, but—"

"Your banishment is lifted. You may visit as often as you'd like. And, you will always be Princess of the Sirens," Dad said and smiled wide, wrinkles forming at the corners of his eyes.

I bowed. "Thank you."

He looked at my mates. "She's all I have left. She's a handful and she's bound to get you into a lot of trouble."

"Rude," I muttered.

"Please, do all you can to keep her safe," Dad said.

"She's not just our mate, but our queen as well," Deryn told him. "We will do everything we can to keep her safe."

Dad nodded, pleased. "Since you are leaving tomorrow, we must have a feast tonight."

He always loved feasts, having them as often as he could when I was a child, so this was no surprise.

"Sam!" Dad yelled.

Sam entered the throne room, having been just outside the doors. "Yes, Your Majesty?"

"Tell everyone we are having a feast tonight! Tell the chef to get to work, immediately."

"You're leaving tomorrow?" Sam guessed.

I nodded. "I need to return home."

He scowled and said no more, turning and marching out to follow Dad's orders.

"Go and rest," Dad said. "I'll have Sam collect you when it's time for the feast."

We all bowed to him, and then walked to my chambers. My body and mind were still reeling from everything that had happened. Plus, I'd used my powers and that had significantly drained me.

We lay on my bed, my head on Rhys's stomach as he slept perpendicular to me. Fox and Deryn slept parallel to me, spooning their bodies to mine, while Nico lay at my feet, hugging them like a teddy bear against his chest.

"Thank you," I whispered to them. "Your memories were just what I needed."

"You need to rest," Fox whispered and stroked my hair.

"You four have no idea how much your love means to me. I don't think I can ever express how much I love you. I owe you so much. You've done so much for me in such a short amount of time."

"And we'll keep doing them, for the rest of our lives," Deryn whispered, his voice groggy with sleep.

"Sleep, my queen. We have plenty of time for everything else. But, you need to recharge," Rhys ordered me, his chest rumbling beneath my head.

THE FEAST AND DANCE AFTERWARDS HAD BEEN A TON OF FUN. WE invited the entire Atlantis population to the royal courtyard and Dad reinstated the merchants' rights to sell once more. It brought some color back, but there was still a lot of work to be done. We ate, drank, and danced, celebrating my mates, the defeat of Brayden, and the new heir.

Leona pulled me aside, near the end of the feast, and held out a leather journal. "You should take this."

At first, I thought it was the journal Brayden had given me, but this one was larger, a true journal size.

"What is it?" I asked as I accepted it.

"Everything we know about empaths. I wrote it all down for you," she said with a smile.

I hugged her. "Thank you, Leona."

"Anything for you, Jojo."

"I'm going to miss you," I whispered into her chest.

"What about me?" Colton asked.

I turned and hugged him. "You too."

"Am I just odd man out? Or are you mad since I'm heir now?" Sam asked.

I giggled and hugged him, then stepped back to look at the three of them. "Thank you, for everything. I couldn't have wished for better friends."

I bowed to them and several people nearby gasped.

"We don't bow to each other," Sam said, parroting something I had said to them as a child.

I stood and held out my hand, palm down and horizontal. "Friends forever."

They placed their hands in a stack atop mine and said in unison, "Friends forever."

We converged for a group hug and I had to wipe my eyes when I stepped back. "Keep each other safe. That's an order from your princess."

They smiled and nodded.

I clutched the journal to my chest and sniffled. "If I stay longer, I'm going to cry."

"Come, my queen," Fox said and draped an arm around my waist. "You need to pack or we won't leave on time tomorrow."

"Until we meet again," Colton said.

My three childhood best friends bowed and left.

"We'll come visit," Fox promised.

I sniffled again and wiped at my eyes. "I know."

Rhys, Nico, and Deryn sat on the floor in my room, talking quietly when we entered.

I sat beside Deryn and leaned my head against his shoulder. "What's up?" I asked.

"We were discussing how your title affects things," Deryn explained.

"Does it?" I asked.

"Yes," Nico said and nodded. "For one, you can't be the human council member."

"Right, since I'm not human."

"You could be the siren council member, but you would need your dad's approval for that," Nico continued.

"I can ask before we leave," I said. I set the journal Leona had written for me in the center of our circle. "Here is everything known about empaths and some general siren knowledge as well."

Nico opened it and began reading. He paused and looked at me over the top of the journal. "This says you have difficulty getting pregnant."

I nodded. "We are almost infertile. One in three sirens are, actually infertile."

He went back to reading.

"I need to pack," I said and stood. A suitcase had been brought to the room for me. I packed the dresses the seamstress had made. They were too beautiful to leave behind. I also packed my copy of the picture Colton kept on his fridge, plus a few trinkets from my childhood.

I put the packed suitcase by the door, then sat in Rhys's lap, leaning my head against his chest.

"Dan destroyed the office," Rhys whispered.

"What? When?"

"When your dad and Trident Douche left with you. He roared and threw a chair through one of the building's windows. Then he broke the table and threw a couple more chairs before Deryn got him to stop."

"You're telling me that Deryn was calmer than Dan?"

Rhys nodded.

"He blamed himself for you being taken," Deryn said. "I haven't seen him lose it like that in a long time."

"My dad and Rhys's dad weren't much better," Fox said. "They were glowing and shifting. I don't think I've ever seen my dad so angry."

"I'd be pretty angry too, if some random guy teleported into what should have been a safe place and interrupted my meeting," I said.

"By contrast, we were pretty calm," Nico said, eyes still glued to the book.

Wow. I knew they were fond of me, but I couldn't believe the kings would be so upset over losing me.

"They were probably mad that Trident Douche had been able to freeze them," I said.

Rhys shook his head. "It was you. They love you like their own daughter."

Three alphas roaring with rage and throwing tantrums when their son's mate was taken. It was a sight I would love to have seen. It was also hard to believe.

"I can show you the video when we get home," Deryn said. "I can see that you still don't believe us fully."

"Would you, if the tables were turned?" I asked.

"I suppose not," he agreed.

"I don't think you're lying," I added. "It's just hard to believe it was because of me."

"You can make people hallucinate," Nico whispered, eyebrows nearly touching his hairline.

"Supposedly, but I wasn't able to do it when training with Leona."

But Leona had been able to do it to me when Brayden took us to the dungeon.

"Scary," Fox whispered. I looked at him and he smiled. "Not you. The power."

"It is my power, it is part of me," I said, stood, and walked to the vanity. Nothing about me had changed physically, but I felt different.

"We'll have to see if we can find an empath to train you," Rhys said.

"There aren't many of us," I explained. "Leona, old lady Anthea, and I are the only ones, as far as I know."

"Maybe we need to offer Leona a job?" Nico asked and looked up at me.

I looked at him in the mirror's reflection. "You're scared of me," I realized, whispering the words because they were painful to say.

"You're powerful, even more so with our powers also at your disposal," he said carefully. "You need training, so you don't accidently do something."

He hadn't denied being scared of me. Wonderful.

Nico set the book down and came to stand behind me. He met my eyes in the mirror. "I'm not scared of you. I'm scared of uncertainty, and your new powers make you an uncertainty. You could enthrall Jinla without meaning to. You could project your nightmares and make us think they are really happening. I'm most worried about you doing something you'll regret and end up wallowing about it. You are a wonderful person and I want to keep you happy and safe as long as I can. I know you would never forgive yourself if you hurt Gavin or one of the others. I'm going to go find Leona."

"He's probably at his or Colton's house in Shelnam," I said.

Nico hugged me from behind and kissed the top of my head. "Okay."

It was hard saying goodbye to my friends and Dad. Nico created a protective shield and we stepped through the portal. Nico's shield kept us from drowning as we entered the undersea cave.

"Pookie!" I yelled, then whistled.

"A Kraken pet," Deryn chuckled. "You should add that to one of your game's storylines."

"That's a good idea," I said seriously, a story already forming in my head.

Pookie swam to us and shrieked in joy when he saw me. He quickly used his magic to surround us and brought us to rest on his head.

I patted him and murmured praises as he swam out of the cave and up the trench. Instead of waiting for our boat, I had Pookie take us all the way to the shore. People screamed and fled the beach. Many took pictures and I couldn't wait for the headline tomorrow in the newspaper.

Pookie used a tentacle to lift me off his head and bring me to his eye level.

"Thank you. You're the best Kraken ever," I said.

Pookie made a cooing noise and set me down on the beach next to my mates, who had leapt off Pookie when he stopped. I waved and Pookie waved a tentacle back before diving into the waters and disappearing.

"Ready?" Fox asked.

"Wait for it," I said, a smirk on my lips as I stared out to sea.

"For what?" Rhys asked, squinting as he looked out.

Pookie shot up and out of the water, his entire body in the air for a moment before he fell back down.

"Goodbye," I whispered and laughed, surprised the Kraken remembered me teaching him to do that.

"Your Highnesses," someone panted behind us.

We turned and looked at the wolf before us, panting hard.

"What is it?" Deryn asked.

"The alpha has lost it. He's destroying your house," the male panted.

Rhys shifted, and we climbed onto his back. As fast as possible, we raced to the pack.

The house was completely destroyed when we arrived and Dan, in warrior form, stood in the rubble howling.

I leapt from Rhys, letting dragon wings form to slow my descent and landed in front of Dan. He looked at me and cocked his head, pausing his howling.

"Dan, what's going on?" I asked.

Martin, Sharla, and the twins stood off to the side, safe, but upset.

Dan growled and walked up to me. "You can't be her. She's gone."

"I'm back," I assured him. "Smell me."

He did and his eyes widened.

"Jolie" he asked. "I heard you were dead."

"From who?" Deryn asked as he came to my side.

Dan pulled Deryn into a bone-crunching hug and shifted back to human form. "Son, you're alive!"

Deryn hugged his dad back. "Dad, what's going on?"

"We received word that you'd been killed in Atlantis. Your bonds are gone," Dan explained. He opened his mouth, then closed it. "No, they're back now."

"Search the compound!" I screamed. "He's here!"

Someone laughed off in the distance. Rhys roared and took off after him, but Brayden had a few tricks up his sleeve. With a burst of light, he disappeared.

Dan pulled me into a hug, inhaling my scent deeply. "I'm sorry, Jolie."

"Why are you apologizing?" I asked, hugging him back.

"We let you get kidnapped. We've become lazy and over-confident."

I patted him. "You have no reason to apologize. They surprised us all. Besides, I needed to go home."

He pushed me back. "So, it's true? You're a siren?"

I nodded. "An empath, actually."

"So, you're Princess Jolie of the Sirens and Four Clans of Jinla?"

"Apparently," I said and sighed. "My life is always so complicated."

Thor and Ezio ran from the gathered pack's mob and hugged me between them. They rubbed their faces against mine silently.

Deryn growled and they both released me.

"Sorry," Thor said and canted his head to the side in submission.

"Jolie, you're okay," Ezio said and hugged me again.

"I am," I assured him.

He released me and looked at Deryn. "No disrespect."

Deryn sighed and rubbed his hand down his face. "She's your alpha female. I get it."

Dan looked at the rubble at his feet. "Guess we're getting a new house." He looked over, meeting my eyes. "I thought I had lost you and Deryn. I thought you were dead."

I thought he had used Leona to make me hallucinate, but this made it apparent that Brayden had the powers of hallucination as well too.

"He's a manipulator," I said. "He makes you do and believe whatever he wants."

Dan asked, "And what about you?"

"Me?"

"You're a manipulator too, right?"

I supposed I was.

"I guess, technically. But, I haven't been able to."

Dan shifted again. "Get off my land."

"What?" I asked, staring in disbelief as Ezio and Thor shifted and growled at me, too.

Tears slid down my cheeks.

"You're no longer welcome here," Dan said, snarling.

No. This wasn't real. Dan wouldn't do this.

I had to be hallucinating.

Closing my eyes, I focused on the magic within me. There, Brayden still had a piece of magic inside my head. He'd camouflaged it well, but now I had it. I squashed it like a bug and opened my eyes.

Dan cradled me in his arms, worry lines marring his forehead.

"Hello, alpha," I whispered.

He rested his forehead against mine. "Daughter, why are you crying?"

I told him, and he wiped my tears away.

"You are pack. Forever," he whispered.

Dan held me for several more minutes, even growling at Deryn when he tried to get close. Everyone left us alone and for the first time, I felt what a father's love should be. My true father loved me and I couldn't blame him for banishing me, since that had been Brayden's doing. Yet, I still hadn't felt true, fatherly love until Dan.

"Where?" Emrys roared.

Dan leaned back and scowled at Emrys who shoved wolves who were too slow to move out of his way. Dan stood, releasing me, and took a step back.

Emrys's eyes were dragon's eyes and smoke billowed out of his nostrils. He growled and Dan backed up more, his hands raised.

"What's going on?" I asked softly, not looking away from Emrys as he approached.

"Same as me," Dan whispered. "His alpha protective urge is in full swing. Someone must have reported your return and he rushed here. Normally, this would be an act of war, but I know what he's going through."

"What is that? What are you going through?" I asked.

"We thought we had lost our daughter. Thought we would never see her again, thanks to our failure to protect her. Her return is something we have to see. We have to smell and touch you to ensure that you are real. We have to know we didn't completely fail and that you are truly here. Truly safe."

"Shouldn't you be happy instead of angry about my return?" I asked. Emrys was almost to me now, his eyes glued to mine.

Dan chuckled. "The fury is for those keeping us from you or trying to take you away."

Emrys stopped before me and reached out a trembling hand. I

151

stepped forward and wrapped my arms around him, my head against his chest.

He inhaled my hair at the top of my head and a single sob broke free before he wrapped me up in his arms and held me silently.

I let him hold me as I had with Dan, letting him absorb my presence.

"Daughter," he whispered. "Are you hurt?"

"I'm fine, Father," I replied and smiled up at him. "I told you I would come back."

He set his hand on my cheek and tears glistened in his eyes. "I thought I'd lost you. I've never lost a child and I thought you would be my first. Those two siren males surprised me and I realized, for all my lectures to you about remaining aware, I was not."

"Dad says he's sorry by the way. He was under mind control, but he still feels bad about breaching your territory," I whispered.

Emrys smiled. "You are back and safe. All else is irrelevant." He looked over my head and scowled. "Dan, what happened to your house?"

"Jolie!" Katar yelled.

"Oh, sure, everyone just breach my territory. No problem," Dan said, throwing his arms in a gesture of frustration, but he smiled at the same time.

"You know why," Emrys said. "Would you have stayed away if she were at my place?"

Dan waved his hand dismissively.

Katar reached for me, still with Emrys's arm around me and Emrys growled.

Katar growled back and began to glow.

"Whoa!" I yelled. "Emrys!"

Emrys stopped snarling and shook his head. "Sorry." He released me and went to stand beside Dan.

"Jolie," Katar whispered.

I turned and bowed. "Your Majesty."

He went to grab me for a hug, but Kara, Katar's mate and Fox's mother, snatched me first, embracing me tightly.

"Jolie," she cried, tears streaming down her face. "You're really back."

Katar growled, and Kara flinched, releasing me quickly so Katar could hug me. "I didn't realize he was so far gone," she whispered.

"I didn't know elves had the same problem," Emrys said.

Kara nodded. "It's very rare, that's why I didn't think about him having it."

Katar held me, then pushed me out to arm's length. "If you ever sacrifice yourself for me, Emrys, or Dan again, I'll lock you in my cells for a month!"

I smiled and said, "I missed you too, Katar."

The rage left him and his shoulders slumped. "Father," he whispered and hugged me again. "You can call me father."

"Do I get to hug her now?" Kara asked with her hands on her hips and one eyebrow arched.

Katar released me to allow his mate to hug me. Kara smacked the back of my head.

"Ouch!" I yelled.

"Stop trying to be the martyr! I'll follow through on Katar's threat. I won't hesitate to lock you up," she said.

"They'll do it," Fox called.

I turned, realizing my mates had stayed back throughout the entire ordeal. They stood beside Martin and his family, watching us while leaning against the wall of the building they stood before.

"Dan, what did you do to your house?" Kara asked.

Dan rubbed the back of his neck sheepishly. "Uh—"

"He decided it needed more bedrooms," I said. "Since I'll be trying to provide an heir or two."

"What?" all four of my mates asked, pushing off the wall and moving towards me.

"I'm not exactly the same person as I was when I left," I explained. "Getting my memories back and truly unlocking my powers has changed me." I looked at the alphas and smiled. "I've decided that I want a little Jolie running around. To see my child spoiled by not just one grandfather, but all of you makes it even more appealing."

"You mean it?" Deryn asked, his eyes alight.

"I can't promise to give you each an heir. I can't even promise to have one, since sirens have low fertility, but I know you will all love my child, no matter who the father is."

Deryn picked me up and crushed his mouth to mine. He set me down and the other three hugged me.

Kara hugged me and whispered, "I may be able to help increase your fertility."

"Okay, but not until we deal with Justina." *And Brayden.* The last thing I needed was to put a child in danger. Plus, there was still the worry of my dhampir war dreams.

"We can wait as long as you want," Fox said.

"She is back, the rumors were true," Johann said, appearing next to Nico.

"Yes, she is," Nico said, since everyone else was too busy glaring at Johann to respond.

"How strong are your empath abilities?" Johann asked.

"I'm powerful, but I don't have the ability to use many of my powers yet," I admitted.

"Would it be better to detain her?" he asked.

"Try it," Dan growled, his eyes turning amber.

Johann raised his hands. "I'm just asking a question."

"She's able to contain her powers," Nico told him.

"We have a teacher coming in a few days," Rhys added.

Johann nodded. "Smart. It's not a good idea to allow an untrained siren to run around."

"Afraid I might ensnare you? Make you like me?" I asked with a scowl.

He smiled, and I was shocked at the difference a smile could make. He looked…fatherly instead of scary.

"I already like you, which I'm sure you know."

I did.

"Your powers were at work from the time you met Rhys," he whispered to me.

"How do you know?" I asked.

He teleported to stand beside me and whispered into my ear, "Because I loathe sirens, yet I can't find any other emotion for you besides admiration. You wanted nothing more than to be loved and here you stand, four princes as your mates and their alphas loving you as if you were their daughter. This isn't a fairy tale and yet you seem to be headed to your happy ever after."

Johann disappeared, leaving me staring at my feet.

He wasn't wrong.

"What did he say?" Nico asked.

"I need a minute," I whispered and backed away from them.

"Jolie," Emrys called my name like you would a child about to do something bad.

"I just need some time. Some space," I said. "I won't leave the wolf lands. Just…give me some space." I let out wings and flew towards the forest, shutting down my bonds with my mates as I searched for a place to think alone. A few miles into the forest, I came to a small waterfall. It had a large boulder at its base, which served as a perfect place to sit. I sat atop it and closed my eyes.

Johann wasn't wrong. This was too good to be true. Yes, bad things had happened, but overall my life was great. Were my powers at work, unbeknownst to me? Was I slowly brainwashing them? Was there a way to reverse it?

"Hello, child," a woman's voice said.

I opened my eyes and my mouth dropped open. A woman floated beside the rock I sat upon, her body see through.

Johann's comment about this not being a fairy tale popped into my head. "Are you my fairy godmother?"

She laughed and said, "I'm your mother, dear."

My mother?

"Siren mother?" I asked.

She scowled. "What other kind is there?"

"Long story, never mind. What are you doing here? Aren't you dead?"

"I bartered with the Goddess to be able to come to you when you most needed me. So, tell me what troubles the Princess of the Sirens?"

"Where do I start?" I sighed.

"What is upsetting you right now?" she asked, sitting down on the rock beside me. I was surprised she didn't pass through it.

"I have four mates and their families love me. Well, most of them. One of them suggested that it might be because my siren abilities were active even without me knowing. That I used my powers to make them fall in love with me."

"We are generally more appealing to others. People do have a tendency to fall for us faster, but it's not a power we control. Sirens are alluring. That's just how we are. We can't stop it."

"What if I did use my powers without knowing?"

"Does it matter now?" she asked. "If they're already your mates, then they must truly love you. Our abilities don't make someone fall in love with us permanently. We would have to keep using our powers constantly or keep them in a trance to do that. You may have unconsciously put out vibes, but you didn't make them fall in love with you."

"How do you know?"

"Because I had the same issues," she said.

"What about making them addicted to you?" I asked. "I was told we could make them crave being around us so much that they become addicted."

She nodded and said, "It can happen. We radiate joy and

people crave that, especially in a world full of darkness. However, it is difficult to make people addicted. I doubt you made anyone an addict because that power is the hardest to learn."

"Mom, I'm afraid. I'm afraid Johann is right, and my powers created this world for me."

Her arm wrapped around me and it felt very real. "I promise that you did not make them fall in love with you. I promise that you are a good person. I can see your soul and it radiates with a goodness necessary for an empath. Keep your heart open and do what you think is right. Your mates love you so much that they interrupted our reunion."

"What?" I asked and looked behind us.

"Who is that?" Fox asked, his voice awed and his eyes wide.

"This is my mother," I whispered and stood.

She stood with me and curtsied. "Hello, Sons. Thank you for keeping her safe. I know you'll continue to do so in the future."

"How are you here?" Nico asked.

"Bartered with the Goddess," she replied. She glided around my mates, looking into each of their eyes and each one, she gave a nod of approval too. "These four will do. I can assure you that their love is true and you didn't bespell them into loving you. Do you have a teacher? He will have to be sure to teach you how to and how not to tamper with their clans' bonds. It is possible for you to tap into them and cause all to become enraged or calm, depending on your desire."

"Leona is coming to teach me," I said, filing away that terrifying possibility for later.

She smiled. "Little Leona. When she was born the entire Kingdom cried, because she *made* us cry. She is one of the strongest empaths I've ever met."

"I'll let her know you approve," I said.

She turned and looked at Nico. "Johann hates sirens. He will never accept us. So, keep an eye on him when Jolie is around. He may like her right now, but his hatred is deep for sirens."

"What happened to make him hate us?" I asked.

She smirked. "He doesn't enjoy losing fights, especially against a young girl who wields no weapons. He doesn't like when people are more powerful than him."

"You fought him?" Fox asked, eyes wide.

"At a Summit Tournament," she replied with a nod.

"Wait, the sirens used to attend?" Rhys asked.

She scowled. "What do you mean *used to*? We've been attending since the Summit was founded."

"They haven't been part of the Summit since we've been attending," Rhys said.

She spun and faced me with a fiery glare. "You tell your father to begin attending again or I will find a way to haunt him."

"I will," I promised, thinking that Brayden must have stopped the sirens from attending the Summit, too.

She mumbled under her breath while looking skyward.

"Mother," I whispered.

Her eyes dropped to mine and she smiled. "There is so much light in you, Jolie. But, there is also darkness. Do not let the darkness take over. If that happens, you may not come back. You have abilities beyond mine. You could destroy the world."

"No pressure," I whispered, my face feeling flushed.

"Boys, you can prevent this by acts of love or even friendship. Keep her happy and safe. If she slips, call her back with your light. Remind her of your love and the things she cherishes. Understand?"

All four princes nodded.

She made a strange sign with her hand and a box popped into existence before her. She held it out to me and said, "This is Selene. She was my familiar. Put her on your forearm and call upon her when you need aid. She's snarky, but powerful."

Inside the box lay a piece of paper, like the one Nar, the nine-tailed fox, had given me, but this had a drawing of a unicorn.

"A unicorn? Are you telling me that this is a real, live unicorn?" I asked, mouth agape.

She smiled and nodded. "She's the last of her kind, as far as I know. They're very powerful. I know she'll be an asset to you."

"Thank you," I said and closed the box's lid.

"You and your mates need to talk," she said. "I love you, Jolie. I wish I had gotten to see you grow up, but I am proud of the woman you are." She kissed me on the cheek, then disappeared.

CHAPTER 12

We didn't talk, instead we opted to go home and nap. Strangely, the four of them opted for their own apartments, leaving me alone in mine. I could tell they weren't mad at me, so I didn't complain nor question them. Sometimes we all needed a little alone time to rejuvenate ourselves, and I totally understood that.

After napping, I popped in an old survival game I hadn't played in years. It was a relatively simple game. The goal was to survive as many days as possible. You had to gather supplies, hunt for food, and defend yourself against monsters on occasion. I had a small base where I had two machines set up that, when I was near them, allowed me to create special gear. I also had a permanent firepit that I just had to add wood to because you had to keep a fire going at night or the monsters would get you. It didn't require a ton of focus, but it still brought a smile to my face.

Deryn walked in a couple hours later and sat behind me, putting his legs outside of mine and letting me rest my back against his chest.

"I haven't seen this game in a long time," Deryn commented and kissed the side of my head. "I used to love this game."

"I love it because it's fun, but relaxing," I said as I picked flowers in the game.

He rubbed my arms gently as I played, and we stayed like that for a half an hour. Then, I turned on a stand-up comedy show I had been wanting to watch. Deryn lay on his side and I lay down in front of him on the couch, scooting back against him so he could wrap his arms around me and cuddle me. It was the first time I'd been able to relax and laugh with just one of them in a while.

"This is nice," Deryn whispered.

I nodded in agreement. It really was.

"Dad really loves you," he whispered. "He was so scared when he thought he'd lost you. He was in so much pain."

"Scared?"

He nodded. "Since your pack bond was locked by Trident Douche, you couldn't feel it. He was so scared. You've become a part of his life, one he looks forward to. The thought that you would no longer be in his life was what really scared him."

Being part of their lives was great and knowing Dan truly cared for me made it even better.

I ordered ten pizzas, then sent a message to the group chat to let the others know.

Deryn continued to cuddle with me until the others came, then he went to my kitchen and grabbed beers for his friends and a cider for me.

Fox sat at my feet and rubbed them while watching the movie I had put on. It was the newest super hero action movie, one we had planned to go see in the theaters, but never got a chance to.

Deryn lifted me so he could sit at my head and let me rest it on his thigh. Rhys and Nico sat on the couch between Fox and Deryn, my body draped across them.

I bolted upright and looked at the couch. "When did you get this?"

It wasn't my couch. My couch had only fit three people at a time. This one had enough room that I could sit between Rhys and Nico without being squished. It was the longest couch I had ever seen.

"Oh, right!" Deryn said and smiled. "I forgot with everything going on, to tell you. This was made by Ezio. He gave it to us as a mating present."

Ezio had started to dabble with furniture making towards the end of our relationship. I'd never seen a finished piece though. It was made from a single log that he'd added cushions to and applied a lacquer to the log that made it shine and prevented us from getting splinters. It shocked me that he had gone out of his way to make something like this for us. It wasn't that long ago that he had disliked Deryn.

"What did my dad say to you?" Nico asked, scowling.

"He's convinced I've been using my powers since I met you. it's the only explanation for my happily-ever-after and him liking me," I said.

"What changed your mind about kids?" Deryn asked.

"When I was young and still living at the palace in Atlantis, I would help out with the babies. I loved taking care of them and wanted lots of kids. When my memories were gone, my life after that was filled with danger and despair. I didn't want to bring a child into that. I don't want to bring a child into that. I want to see you playing with your children and see our kids with their grandparents. Your clans have been at war, yet I know they would cherish them and spoil them, even if they aren't their biological grandchildren. I hope I'm able to have children and I hope I can have one for each of you, but first, we need to find and kill Justina and Brayden."

"We will," Rhys promised.

The doorbell rang and Fox answered it, getting our pizzas

from the delivery man, and set them on the coffee table. We all eagerly dug in and watched the movie. I sat between Nico and Rhys on our giant couch and relaxed. There were lots of things I could worry about, but now wasn't the time to worry about them. Now was the time to enjoy our peace, no matter how temporary it might be. If this adventure had done anything, it had made me realize that I needed to cherish the time I had with my mates. Our lives were chaotic at best and I never knew when me or my mates might get separated.

THE FOUR SITES ON THE SCREEN LOOKED VERY SIMILAR, BUT THEIR location was the most important factor. Two of them were close to the dragon's den, too close.

"Not those two," I said and pointed out the ones I was discussing.

Dan nodded and made a note on his paper.

The four alphas had made me part of their council, as the siren representative, and today was my first meeting. True to their word, they'd been working on my academy suggestion. One of these sites would be the school's location and once I chose, the big planning would begin.

I stared at the map with the two remaining sites' locations marked. One was in the center of the city near the park I had returned their necklace at. The other was in a warehouse district.

"This one. It's near food, a park, and has more transportation options," I said and pointed at the one by the park.

They nodded in agreement and Dan made more notes.

"We obtained some copies of rules and regulations handbooks from several schools. I'd recommend highlighting rules you want added to your school's handbook and writing new ones as well. Once you have these prepared, we will all review and make our own suggestions," Johann said.

He handed me ten booklets, and I set them on the growing stack of documents I had to take home.

Rhys opened a new presentation and put it on the large screen in front of us. "Here are a few options for the architecture," he said. "I can modify them if you need something changed."

He scrolled through a few.

"Stop!" I yelled as he moved to the fifth slide. "This one," I whispered. The drawing called to me and it took me a minute to realize why. "You incorporated something from each of the four clans in this one. It's perfect."

He pulled out the paper copy and handed it to Dan who looked at it closely, then passed it to the other alphas.

"Vote?" Dan asked after they'd all looked at it.

"Approved," the other three alphas said.

"Rhys, you are cleared to begin in depth work on this one," Dan said.

"Understood," Rhys replied and took the paper back.

"Any other business?" Dan asked.

No one spoke up.

"Today's meeting is adjourned," Dan said and stood up with a groan and stretched.

The other alphas stood as well and packed up their papers. I looked at my stack and sighed. So much work.

"Ready, princess?" Rhys asked and added my documents to his stack.

I nodded and waved to the alphas. "See you later."

They waved back, and Rhys and I headed out of the office and down to the SUV where Thor waited for us. He hugged me and bumped his fist with Rhys's before climbing into the driver's seat.

"How was your first meeting?" Thor asked.

"I've got homework," I muttered, but honestly didn't feel bad. I was excited to get this school started and for the kids to learn about each other and actually be ready to go out into the world and interact with any race.

"What's on the agenda for the rest of the night?" Rhys asked.

"I have to work on my story proposal," I said.

"For your game proposal?" Rhys asked.

I nodded. It was the first time that I had come up with my own story idea and planned to pitch it to the company. To say I was nervous was a gross understatement.

"Aren't you going to the tournament tonight?" Thor asked.

"What tournament?" I asked back.

Please don't let it be more fighting. I had had enough with fighting tournaments. Not that I doubted my mates, but I just wasn't ready for more trouble.

"The huge video game tournament," he said, looking at me in the rearview mirror.

"FighterCon? FighterCon is tonight!" I screamed and pulled out my phone. How could I have forgotten about the biggest video game tournament in the country?

I checked the clan group chat and almost squealed out loud. Three of them were on planes right now, headed to Jinla.

"They're coming!" I screamed.

"Who?" Rhys asked.

"Dragon, Orphan, and Turbo! They're on their way now," I explained.

"Wait, your video game clan members are going to be here in person?" Rhys asked.

"I told you guys about this months ago," I reminded him.

"I'd forgotten with everything that happened," he whispered and gazed out the window.

I sent a text to the clan: Can't wait to see you!

Thor dropped us off and promised to come pick us up at five to take us to the convention center.

I tapped my foot anxiously as the elevator went up to my floor and Rhys chuckled.

"What?" I asked him.

"You're like a kid waiting to get candy."

"It's been years since I last saw them!" I explained. "And, I haven't been able to play online as much either. So, I'm super excited."

"I can't wait to meet them," Rhys said and smiled. He set down the stack of documents he had been carrying on the floor of the elevator.

"What?" I asked. I hadn't planned on introducing my clan to my mates. Not that I cared or didn't want them to meet. It just wasn't part of the plan.

He arched a brow. "Planning to ditch us for your friends?"

I rolled my eyes at him. "No, I just hadn't thought about it. Last FighterCon we met at, I had been single and my life wasn't always in danger. So, I didn't think about you guys coming this time."

"We're going," he said and folded his arms across his chest.

I got distracted by his biceps a moment, then met his eyes. "Okay. I wasn't trying to ditch you. I really just didn't think about it."

"You don't think about us?" Fox asked behind me and clutched his heart.

I rolled my eyes at him and walked out of the elevator. "You guys are ridiculous sometimes."

Fox pecked me on the cheek and smiled. "You love us."

I smiled. I did love them.

"What's got her all frazzled?" Fox asked, following beside Rhys as we walked to my apartment.

"She's got a big convention tonight and her clan members are coming. She wasn't planning on introducing us," Rhys said.

"That's not what I said!" I snapped.

Rhys smirked, and I realized that he was messing with me. I gave him my best glare and reached for my door handle, but it was suddenly not there. I fell sideways into Deryn who just laughed.

"It's nice to see you, too," he said and hugged me.

I stood on tiptoe and kissed his cheek. "Hello, Moon Moon."

"That's a big stack of crap," Deryn commented as Rhys walked in.

"Showering!" I yelled to them and ran to the bathroom. I could hear them talking and laughing and smiled as I turned the shower on.

"Mind if I join you?" Nico asked.

I screamed and spun around with scales covering my body.

He laughed so hard that he doubled over and clutched at his stomach.

I punched his shoulder as hard as I could with my dragon scale covered hand. "You jerk!"

He rubbed his shoulder but didn't look regretful at all. "You should be able to sense me teleporting near you with our bond. I shouldn't be able to startle you like that."

"I still can't quite figure out how to use the bonds," I admitted and looked down at my feet.

"It's okay. It takes some getting used to. I can help you. First, let's get in the shower so we aren't late," Nico said.

I nodded and stripped quickly before climbing into the shower. He climbed in behind me and wrapped his arms around me, pressing his body against mine as we stood under the warm water.

"I missed you today," he whispered in my ear.

"I missed you too," I said and rubbed one of his forearms that was latched around me, just below my breasts.

"What are your plans tomorrow?" he asked.

"Hanging out with the clan for a bit, most likely," I said.

"Well, how about I take you out for a dinner date? Just you and me."

I turned around and wrapped my arms around his shoulders,

linking my fingers behind his head. "That sounds wonderful. Where are we going to go?"

"Wherever you want," he said and kissed the tip of my nose.

While I thought about what I wanted, he tilted my head back to get my hair in the water and rubbed it a bit so it got completely wet, then he added shampoo and lathered me up.

"I'll let you know tomorrow," I said. "I can't think about tomorrow's food yet."

He rinsed my hair out and then washed his hair while I soaped up my body. "How was the meeting?" he asked.

"Good. I'm really excited about this school. I think it's going to be really good for the kids," I said, then playfully pushed him with my hip out of the water so I could rinse.

"It's a great idea. I can't wait to see how it goes," he said.

"Nico, is there something bothering you?" I asked him.

He scowled a moment, then sighed. "Yeah. I had an argument with my dad."

"About me," I guessed.

He nodded. "He really hates sirens."

"Well, I can't change what I was born as. It's not like I chose to be a siren or an empath," I grumbled.

"I know. He's just an ass," he said. He pushed me back against the wall of the shower, putting a hand on either side of my head. "And I don't care what he says. You're fucking perfect."

"I'm far from perfect, but I appreciate the compliment," I said and kissed him on the lips softly.

"I wish I could show you how I see you," he whispered and kissed my neck. "You're perfect for me, Jolie."

Him and three other guys.

"And it makes sense that you would be perfect for the others as well," he said, as though he heard my thought. "We all like pretty much the same things, so us all liking you isn't much of a stretch."

"Does it make it less romantic for me to say that you're all perfect for me?" I asked and bit my lower lip.

He focused on it and groaned. "Stop teasing me, you butt. We have to get out and we don't have time for fun."

"Sorry," I said and chuckled. "I wasn't doing it to tease you."

"And no, it doesn't make it less romantic," he replied and shut off the water.

"Hurry up!" Deryn called through the door. "Your pizza is getting cold."

After drying off, I walked out of the bathroom, naked, since I hadn't brought a change of clothes with me.

All eyes turned to me and I stared in shock at a male I didn't know standing in the living room. His eyes were not on mine, focused a bit lower.

Nico set his hand on me and teleported us to my bedroom.

"Who is that?" I asked and knew I was blushing.

"He is a friend of Rhys's from the architectural company he works for," Nico said. "He's a huge gamer too, so he is going to go with us."

"Well, he definitely got an eyeful," I grumbled and dug through my drawers for some clean underwear.

"Sorry, I didn't know he was here or I would have teleported us to the room from the bathroom," Nico said.

I waved my hand dismissively. "It's fine. He's not the first person to see me naked on accident."

"I don't want to know," Nico said and sighed.

I laughed and got my underwear, pants, and bra on, then stared into my closet. I had more than a dozen geeky shirts and I couldn't decide which one I wanted to wear tonight.

"Tough decision?" Nico asked.

I looked at him over my shoulder. He was dressed now, probably teleporting to his apartment to grab clothes and then back again while I stared at my closet. "Yes, it is."

"Can I pick for you?" he asked.

"Sure," I said and stepped back.

He smiled and looked at each of my shirts, then shuffled through them again one more time before making his selection. It was a shirt that said, "Not all maidens need saving."

"Not sure this applies to me," I grumbled. "I seem to always need saving."

"You didn't need saving when you fought against Rhys's mom," he reminded me.

"I needed saving from Trident Douche," I snarled and tugged the shirt on over my head.

He rested his hand against my cheek and whispered, "It hurt so much when we realized that you didn't know who we were. I wanted to slaughter everyone in Atlantis, I was so mad."

Nico wasn't prone to bouts of rage, so his statement surprised me.

"I'm glad you didn't," I said and set my hand atop his on my cheek.

He kissed me and then rubbed our noses side to side. "Me too."

Rhys walked in and said, "Sorry about that. I should have warned you he was coming over."

"It's fine," I assured him and went to my dresser to grab my hair brush.

Fox walked in and grabbed the brush from me. "Let me."

I sat and let him brush my hair. Rhys and Nico went out to the living room, leaving me alone with Fox.

"How was your day?" I asked him.

He brushed out my hair slowly, being sure to get all of the tangles. "It was fine. I made some new charms and mom is going to sell them."

"Nice," I said softly, my body completely relaxing with Fox being with me and brushing and stroking my hair like he was.

"Is there anything I should know about your clan members?" he asked and set the brush down. His fingers wove into my hair and he began to braid it.

"Not really. They're homebodies like me, but they are good people."

"Races?" he asked.

"Oh, uh..." I thought about it and said, "Human. They're all human." I hadn't really thought about them all being human until now.

"Are you going to tell them that you aren't human?" he asked, releasing my hair now that it was braided.

"I don't know," I admitted. "I mean, if they ask I won't lie, but I don't want to just bust out with, 'hey, guess what? I'm not human.' It would be a bit weird."

He shrugged. "I don't know your friends, so I can't say for sure. Just know that we don't care."

I stood and kissed him. "I know, Kit." I had started calling him Kit, since he turned into a fox and was childlike most of the time.

"Ready?" he asked.

I nodded, and we walked out to the living room. I snatched a slice of pizza from the almost empty box and ate it quickly. "Sorry about earlier," I told the guy. I still didn't know his name.

He stood, and I almost took an involuntary step back. He was tall, like super tall.

He held out his hand and smiled. "It's alright. I'm sorry I startled you. I'm Austin. I work with Rhys."

I shook his hand and grimaced immediately. Vampire. He was a vampire.

He dropped my hand and stepped back quickly.

"What was that?" Rhys asked, concerned.

"She's been a vampire's donor," Austin said. "Other vampires can read it from touching her."

"I wasn't a donor," I growled.

He dipped his head in a sign of apology.

"Is he talking about that vampire we killed in the park?" Fox asked.

"No, this one is still alive," Austin said.

Damn him. He just didn't know when to shut up.

"Jolie," Deryn growled.

"I've got to keep some secrets, so you'll still think I'm interesting," I said with a wide smile, trying to play it off.

Nico sighed and looked up at the ceiling. "There is always something new to learn about you."

"I'm mysterious like that," I said and wiggled my fingers at him.

"Do we need to kill this vampire?" Deryn asked.

"I don't think so," I said.

"It's not a claiming mark," Austin said. "It's just something vampires can sense when they touch her. It's like a mark, but it's nothing serious."

"I think we should kill him," Rhys said and Deryn nodded.

"Not tonight," I said and grabbed another slice of pizza. "I've got games to play and friends to see."

"We've got a bit of time, so don't choke that down so fast. You have time to actually chew it," Deryn said.

I didn't respond to him, but did slow down.

Everyone took seats around the room and I pulled out my phone, checking my messages.

Dragon: I have arrived!

Turbo: me too

Orphan: Psh. I've been here. You're all late.

Me: I'll be there around 5:20. I'm bringing some people with me.

Turbo: You have friends?

Orphan: Aw, I thought we were your only friends.

Dragon: More souls for me to consume in battle!

Me: You all better be on your best behavior.

All three sent back, "LOL."

This night could turn out to be very interesting.

I scrolled through the news sites, seeing what the headlines were and stopped at a picture of us riding Pookie. "Hey, look." I showed everyone the picture.

"Is that a Kraken?" Austin asked.

"His name is Pookie. And yes."

His eyes widened, and he gaped at me. "You're the siren princess everyone is talking about! Holy shit! I didn't realize she was the one you guys are mated to."

"Wasn't that headline news when my dad picked me up?" I asked.

Nico nodded. "Front page of every paper. Jolie, savior of the four clans is also Princess of the Sirens."

It was possible my clan already knew I wasn't human then. I scrolled through some more, then stopped at an article about Nico with a picture of him and a beautiful woman. The headline was asking whether he was cheating on me or not.

"Did you see this?" I asked Nico and showed him my phone.

He snatched it out of my hand and sighed. "Seriously? They seriously put an article in here about this?"

"We need to talk?" I asked him with an arched eyebrow.

He looked at me and gave me his famous stare. "Really?"

I smiled and took my phone back. "Just checking."

"You know we'd kick his ass," Fox said.

"Actually, I don't. Guys are always looking out for each other. You might cover for him," I countered. I knew Nico hadn't done anything. I trusted him, but I could also sense his feelings through our bonds, so I knew how he felt. If he had been cheating on me, I would have felt his sexual arousal and release through the bond.

Nico shook his head and smiled. "I am so glad you're not a normal girl."

"I should be offended by that statement, but I'll take it as a compliment," I told him and winked.

Austin laughed and said, "I can see why you like her, Rhys."

"Are you going to play any of the games?" Fox asked me.

I nodded. "There are two that we always play. I suck at them, but I do better than most of the scrubs who show up. And a third game that I play every single tournament I can."

"You may have your hands full this time," Rhys said. "Austin is a pretty good gamer."

I looked at him and said, "We'll see. I'm always up for a new battle."

He smiled. "Challenge accepted."

They chatted a bit more and then it was finally time to go. We piled into the SUV with Austin up front beside Thor. Thor looked back at me, and I smiled. Yeah, I knew he was a vampire. I was good.

"Ready?" Thor asked.

I nodded. "Let's go!"

The guys chatted amongst themselves while I stared out the window. Having four mates wasn't normally an issue, but I was worried that being royalty was going to cause problems tonight. If it had just been me, I could have disguised myself so I wouldn't be noticed, but there was no disguising them. They were easy to spot because they stood out no matter where they were. Who knew having hot mates would cause trouble?

"We are going to go in through the back, so we can avoid the media hounds," Thor advised us.

"Sweet," I said, despite knowing that the people inside would be a problem as well.

"You're worried about something," Nico whispered in my ear.

"Just worried we're going to cause trouble because we're royalty," I said. "Normally I walk around and only those who know me from being part of the gaming community talk to me. Now, people are likely to stop us because of being royals. I just don't know if I can handle it."

Being in big crowds wasn't my favorite, but when it was a large group of people who loved the same thing as me, in this case video games, it was easier. Now, I didn't know what would happen. I had no idea what to expect.

CHAPTER 13

We made it all of ten feet before my mates were recognized. There weren't usually many women at FighterCon, but there were still more than a hundred. And as we entered the main room, a dozen women rushed towards us.

"That's my cue to leave," I said and slipped away, weaving my way through the crowd until I made it to the sign-up sheets.

"Hello," the volunteer at the table said with a friendly smile. She was young, eighteen years old at the most, but exuded power. She was a mage, but I'd never met someone who leaked magic power like her.

"Hi, I'd like to sign up for some of the tournaments," I told her.

She held out a pen and waved at the six clipboards with papers on them before her. "All sign-ups are still open. Just put your gamertag and your cell number, in case we need to contact you."

"Thanks," I told her and took the pen, filling out the sign-ups I chose. After finishing, I gave her back the pen and looked at the main stage where many others were gathering, but no battles had started yet.

She looked at my name on the sign-up sheet nearest her and her eyes widened. "You?" she whispered. She put her fingers in her mouth and whistled loudly.

The announcer, who had been midsentence, stopped and turned to look at her. His eyes locked with mine and he smiled wide.

Uh oh. Whenever Nathan, the announcer, got that look, there was going to be a huge ordeal. Having his gaze on me made me very nervous.

"The Princess of Fighters is here!" Nathan told the crowd.

I hated that nickname. He'd coined it when I won the first year.

"Our StreetBrawler champion, two years running, has just arrived. Come on up here, Jo!"

The crowd cheered, and I groaned. He'd done this last year too. Damn him.

After climbing the stairs, I walked to the center of the stage where Nathan stood. I waved to the crowd with a smile, ignoring the jeers since most were friendly goads.

"We were worried you weren't going to make it, Jo," Nathan said.

"Why is that?" I asked.

"We weren't sure if a Princess would be allowed to come," he explained.

"Gaming is my first love," I replied and smiled wide. "Plus, my mates are with me."

"Think you can retain your title of Champion?" he asked.

"I'm ready to find out," I answered, and the crowd cheered. Looking out at the audience, I saw my clan members standing together in the front. I jumped down off the stage and hugged the three of them.

"What took you so long?" Orphan teased. He smiled down at

me with dark brown eyes that twinkled with mischief. He was always full of mischief and puns. His puns were epic.

"And what's with the huge entourage?" Dragon asked.

"Being a princess causes a lot of problems when I go out in public," I said with a shrug.

"Can't you sing them away or something?" Turbo asked. He was the shortest of the group, though taller than me. He had brown hair that was so dark, it looked black. He also had the longest and thickest eyelashes I'd ever seen on a man. I was jealous of them, personally.

"You guys know about me being a siren?" I asked.

The trio nodded.

"Everyone knows," Dragon said. "It was on every news outlet."

"Well, I don't have true siren abilities, so I couldn't sing them away," I said with a laugh.

"Jo!" Orphan yelled and pulled me into his chest.

I looked back over my shoulder. Rhys knelt with his knee in a guy's back on the ground behind me.

"Hey, babe," Rhys said to me.

"What…"

"That guy was about to hit you," Orphan explained and released me.

Rhys smiled at Orphan. "Thanks for moving her."

Orphan smirked. "I can't lose my teammate right before a match."

I punched his arm and he laughed.

Rhys let the guy up and I asked, "Fern, are you ever going to get over this grudge?"

Fern was a little older than me and had been Champion the year before I won. Now, he hated me. He wasn't truly dangerous. Just a bit of a drunken idiot.

"I hate you," he growled.

Rhys growled and Fern flinched away. "You try to hurt my mate again and I'll do more than knock you down. Got it?"

Fern nodded and pushed off into the crowd.

"He's one of your mates?" Turbo asked.

I nodded. "Guys, this is Rhys. Rhys, this is Orphan, Turbo, and Dragon."

He shook their hands, but looked at Dragon the longest, for the second time that day having to look up at someone, since Dragon was seven feet tall. "What are you, a third dragon?" Rhys asked.

"Quarter," Dragon answered. "No shifting, sadly."

"You would have made one hell of a dragon," Rhys said with a wide smile.

"Psh, I am an awesome dragon."

Dragonknight was part dragon? I'd never known that. I thought he was human the whole time.

"There you are," Fox said, squeezing between two guys to get to me. "Look, I got you a gift." He held out a keychain that had my favorite female fighter from the game *Underlook*. She had a mechanical rabbit she used to stomp on people and also had a shield to protect teammates.

I took it and squealed. "Thank you!" I kissed Fox and put the keychain in my pocket.

"Mate two?" Turbo asked.

I nodded and introduced them.

We watched the matches, chatting about them, and I felt like myself. Finally.

Nico slid up behind me and wrapped his arms around my waist. I leaned back against him as I watched Dragon fighting Deryn on *Street Brawler*. Deryn was a decent player, but there was no way he could beat Dragon.

"You look happy," Nico whispered in my ear. "It's a good look on you."

I linked my fingers with his where they lay on my stomach and said, "I am happy."

Deryn lost, but he didn't get mad like usual. He actually

laughed and shook hands with Dragon. He jogged over and kissed my cheek before heading off towards one of the other gaming areas.

"Jo versus Austin!" Nathan announced.

I patted Nico's hands, and he released me. I jogged up the steps and held my hand out to Austin, ready this time since I knew what he was.

He shook my hand and said, "I've been looking forward to this."

"Hopefully I won't disappoint you," I said and took the chair on the right I picked up the controller and chose my character.

Nathan was providing commentary, but I tuned him out. The only thing that mattered was the game. Focused on the screen, I debated my first move. I had no idea what Austin's play style was like. But, I decided to start off aggressive, since that wasn't how I usually played. If he knew about me or had seen me play before, he would expect me to block and wait for him to attack.

The match started, and I sent a flaming ball across the screen. He had started to rush me and hadn't prepared for my attack, so it hit his character.

The crowd erupted.

Pushing forward, we exchanged blows, but I was able to block or parry most of his. He jumped up and I smiled. Noob. Hitting the buttons in the correct order, I activated my characters super. My character jumped up, hitting his in the jaw, then delivered seven more punches midair before throwing him across the screen. His character hit the ground and died.

I didn't avert my eyes from the screen as I waited for the second round to start. This time, I waited for him to make the first move. He surprised me by dashing across the screen and grabbing me, then tossing me backwards. As soon as I landed, I leapt up and sent a fire ball at him. He parried it and stood, waiting. Challenging me.

Fireball. Parry. Fireball. Parry. Super fireball. I smiled smugly, but that disappeared as he parried all four hits of the super fireball.

Son of a bitch!

He was good and before I knew it, he defeated me.

Shit.

Tied one to one, this next match would decide the winner.

Our fight was intense and I was losing. I had one ace up my sleeve and it was time to use it. He activated his super and I parried every hit, then activated my super. He lost to a crowd screaming in disbelief. He set his controller down and exhaled loudly while running his hand through his hair.

I turned and held out my hand. "Good game."

He shook my hand and smiled. "Thanks. You too."

The next contestants climbed onto the stage, so I hopped down.

Deryn and Fox high fived me.

"You almost lost," Dragon said. "You need to play more."

"You're rusty as fuck," Turbo said and laughed.

"I won," I said and shrugged.

"That was a nice move," Orphan said.

I smiled and turned to watch the next contestants.

After a few uneventful bouts, Nathan announced the next match and I knew I was doomed.

"Dragon versus Jo!"

"Well, I'm dead," I whispered to Nico.

He kissed my cheek and said, "Just go have fun. Who cares if you win or not?"

He was right. I just needed to have fun. I climbed up the steps and sat in the chair.

Dragon sat down and said, "You better try your hardest."

I rolled my eyes. "Duh."

We looked at our screens and waited for the match to start. He was an aggressive fighter usually, but I just wanted to have fun. So, I ran at him and did a spinning kick. He blocked it and punched me with a hard uppercut that took half my health.

I danced backwards and hit the crouch and then stand buttons multiple times to taunt him.

He let out a booming laugh, then dashed across the screen and hit me with an eighteen-hit combo that ended round one.

He charged me at the beginning of round two and I did everything I could to block or parry his hits. I was successful for a bit, but tried to punch him and he caught me, throwing me back into the corner and began juggling my body with kicks.

"Dammit! Stop juggling me!" I yelled with a wide smile.

He stopped, then squatted and punched me once in the shin, killing me.

"Dragon wins!" Nathan yelled.

We shook hands and climbed off the stage, laughing.

"I'm going to go play *Dank Souls*," Orphan said.

"I'm up soon for *Soulsbourne*," Dragon said and headed in that direction.

"Are you playing in the *Dank Souls* tournament?" Nico asked.

I shook my head. "No. I was going to do the *Soulsbourne*, but I'm super rusty." Even if I would never admit it to Turbo.

"Let's check out the vendors," Deryn suggested. He took my hand and pushed his way through. I followed behind him until we cleared the crowd.

We walked side by side down the vendor stalls, pausing to look at various items. We were halfway down the second aisle when I stopped and turned around. "You're taking turns, aren't you?"

"What?" Deryn asked, setting down the *Dank Souls* figurine he had been looking at.

"You guys are taking turns being with me tonight," I said.

He nodded. "Yeah."

"Why?"

"We all talked and agreed that we don't get enough alone time with you. So, we decided to take turns. Doesn't matter if it's five minutes or a full day, we just want to prioritize one-on-one time with you."

"Because I want that?" I asked.

"No," he said and pulled me into his arms. "Because *we do*." He kissed me, then smiled. "You always look so beautiful when you're happy."

Pushing away from him, I continued down the aisles with his hand in mine. He stopped me to look at something and I leaned into his side. Ever since we'd mated, Deryn had calmed down and reverted back to the happy and playful guy I'd met. I was so happy to have him back.

"Moon Moon," I said to get his attention.

He looked at me with a smirk. "Yes?"

"Do we have an anniversary date?"

He frowned and thought about it a moment. "I suppose the day you asked us to be your mates would count."

"Would you prefer to have separate anniversary dates? To use the dates that I mated with you instead?"

"I don't know," he said and shrugged. "I hadn't really thought about it."

"Well, just think about it," I said. Turning, I spotted a figurine I'd been searching for for years. I rushed over and picked it up. "Yes!"

The seller was helping someone else, so I waited patiently for my turn. Deryn wandered over and looked at the figurine. "Isn't that the one you've been looking for?"

I nodded.

"How can I help you?" the seller, a middle-aged man with grey hair and a grey beard asked.

"I'd like to buy this," I said and held out the figurine towards him.

"Three hundred dollars," he said.

"Three hundred? It sold for sixty," I growled.

"Yeah, originally it sold for that, but now it's a collector's item and hard to find," he said. "Three hundred is my price."

Dammit. I didn't want to spend that much, but I really wanted the figurine.

"We'll take it," Deryn said and held out his credit card.

"Deryn," I grumbled.

The seller boxed it up and handed it to Deryn. "Thank you for your business. Have a great day."

"Why did you do that?" I asked him.

"You wanted it. You've been looking for this thing for months. It's a gift, so accept it gratefully."

"Thank you," I said and hugged him. "Thank you."

He smiled and kissed me. "Anything for you, baby."

"Hey," Rhys said, meeting us at the end of the vendors.

"Hello," I replied. "What have you been up to?"

"I watched a few battles and played some of the demos set up," he said.

"I'm going to go find Fox," Deryn said and took my figurine with him.

Rhys held out his hand. I threaded my fingers with his and we headed back to the *Street Brawler* tournament. Normally I had issues getting through the crowds, but Rhys easily made his way, pulling me after him. We got a spot at the front and Rhys pulled me around to stand in front of him. He draped his arms over my shoulders and rested his chin atop my head. Relaxed and at peace.

Having them like this was great. Having my mates calm and happy made me happy.

I just hoped it would last.

"It's the final round!" Nathan announced. "Dragon versus Octane!"

Octane? He had dropped off the gaming world a few years ago. He was great, though a little intense.

The battle was relentless and long. They almost went to time, both of the first two rounds. They each won one round, so this one would decide the winner.

Dragon looked calm as ever, but so did Octane.

Turbo and Orphan found us in the crowd and came to stand by me.

"This is a great match so far," Turbo said.

I nodded.

The third round started and neither player moved. There was a tense silence for thirty seconds, and then Dragon moved. They battled magnificently, hitting, blocking, parrying, and yet they remained even on health. They continued battling, then Octane activated his super. The crowd filled with loud yells of, "Oh!".

But, the super missed somehow.

Dragon activated his super and that was it. He won the match.

The crowd went wild and I joined them, screaming and clapping.

Dragon got his trophy and check from Nathan, then yelled, "I am victorious!"

We chuckled, then I hugged him when he made it down to us. "That was awesome!" I told him.

"Luck," Orphan said. "How did his super miss?"

Dragon shrugged. "Scrub mistake? Whatever, I won."

"Let's celebrate!" Orphan said. "There's got to be a bar nearby."

"There's one just across the block," Rhys said.

"To the bar!" Dragon shouted.

We began walking toward the exit and Rhys whistled loudly. Nico teleported to me, making Turbo jump back in surprise. Deryn jogged over with Fox at his side, their hands full of new bags.

"What did you buy?" I asked curiously.

"No peeking!" Fox said and hid the bags behind his back.

Following Dragon and Rhys, we walked into the bar Rhys had

mentioned, but Dragon, Orphan, Turbo, and I stopped immediately.

The bar was closer to an opera house than a bar. There were hardly any people inside and the ones who were there were obviously much older than us.

"Let's go somewhere else," I suggested.

"What's wrong with this place?" Rhys asked.

"I didn't bring my top hat and monocle with me," Turbo said and my clan laughed.

"There's a great dive bar two blocks away," I told everyone. "Let's head there."

"A dive bar? You *want* to go to a dive bar?" Fox asked, scowling.

"I'd rather not pay fifteen for a beer," Orphan said with a scoff.

"Come on," I prompted them and went back outside.

They followed, but Rhys, Fox, and Nico were scowling and talking amongst themselves too quietly for me to hear several feet back from us. Through the bond, I sensed that they were confused, but nothing else.

The dive bar had loud music and several people outside were smoking.

We showed the bouncer our IDs, except for the princes who just walked by him like he didn't exist. He didn't stop them.

Once inside, we went to the bar to get our drinks.

"Turbo paid two years ago and last year was Orphan," I said. "So, looks like it's my turn."

The bartender was a beautiful woman with flowing hair. She ignored us to look at the princes. "What can I get you, Your Highnesses?"

Deryn stepped up behind me and put his hands on my shoulders. "What do you want, love?"

Her eyes widened as she looked at me then him but didn't say anything.

"Four beers for us, then whatever you guys want," I said, feeling annoyed.

"There's a bench table outside big enough for all of us," Turbo said. "I'll go snag it."

"I'll come with you," I said and followed him out to the back patio. There were about ten people in the back, but most were sitting at the small tables with groups of two to four.

We sat at the table and Turbo turned to me. "You sure you're happy with those guys?" he asked.

"Yeah, why?"

"You just don't seem like you have much in common."

"We do. They play games just not as much as us."

"You mated with filthy casuals?" he asked in mock horror.

I laughed and nodded. "Yeah."

"They seem to legit care about you."

"Yeah? You can tell after four hours?" I teased.

He nodded. "They spent the whole night making sure you were happy. They stayed with you, but not to try to keep guys away, just because they like you."

"You can tell all that?"

He smirked. "I'm pretty perceptive, even if I tend to run head-long into battles."

Nico teleported behind me and Turbo cursed. "Could you stop that? You're going to give me a heart attack."

Nico smirked. "Sorry." He set down a mug of beer for me and one for Turbo.

The others joined us with their own beers. I raised mine and the others followed. "Congrats, Dragon!"

"Congrats!" everyone said.

We drank and talked for hours. It was well past midnight when we decided to leave. I hugged my clan and said goodbye as they climbed into a taxi.

My mates stood several feet away, leaning against the bar's wall, just watching me.

"What?" I asked and stumbled towards them, giggling. I was both drunk and exhausted.

"You're different with them," Rhys said.

"What? How?" I didn't try to act different.

"You didn't stop smiling the entire time we were here. Even when you were complaining about a game, you didn't stop smiling," Deryn said.

"We never talk about anything serious. Our entire relationship is based on having fun. We use each other to escape from reality most of the time," I explained.

They hadn't moved from their spots against the wall of the building. So, I walked to them, standing just in front of the quad. "Let's go home. I'm tired and I drank more than I should have."

"Okay," Fox said and picked me up. "Let's go home."

CHAPTER 14

"Jolie, put the knife down," Fox whispered with his hands held out placatingly.

Knife? When had I picked up a knife? We'd walked home from the bar and…that was the last thing I remembered, coming home from the bar.

"Something's wrong," Deryn whispered.

"I can see that," Fox snapped.

"Jolie," Rhys said.

I turned and faced him, adjusting my grip on the kitchen knife.

"Put it down," he ordered me, using his alpha voice.

"That shit doesn't work on me!" I snapped.

"Time to sleep," Nico whispered behind me.

I spun, but he put his hand over my mouth and covered my face with the cloth he held. I had no choice but to inhale, and the chloroform did its job and knocked me unconscious.

Brayden had been right, they were trying to control me.

The effects didn't last long, but it was long enough for them to tie me up and transport me to the wolf den. They had put me in a containment cage meant to hold loup wolves, wolves who had lost their humanity and were crazed and attacked anything and everything.

"Let me go!" I screamed and struggled against my restraints.

Nico, Fox, Rhys, Deryn, and Dan stood outside the cage, all scowling.

"Mind control," Dan said. "Which means that asshole is nearby."

"Not necessarily," Rhys whispered. "She told me he was able to communicate telepathically with her. He could be doing this from far away."

"How do we stop it?" Fox asked.

I turned my skin into scales and snapped the ropes holding my arms. "Let me out!" I screamed and breathed fire.

Nico put up a barrier around the cage, keeping the fire safely away from them.

Those jerks were going to pay for imprisoning me!

"I am Princess Jolie of the Sirens!" I yelled at them. "Release me or you will be declaring war!"

"How long until Leona gets here?" Deryn asked.

"Tomorrow was what she said," Fox answered.

The bars of the cage were made with extremely strong metal. How could I escape? How could I get out of here?

"When did this start?" Dan asked, moving closer to the cage.

I shifted into a wolf and snapped my teeth at him.

He scowled and his eyes shone gold. "Sit," he ordered me.

My body trembled, but I held my head up higher and growled. No. I would not obey him.

"I'm not shielding her," Deryn said.

"It started when we got back from the bar," Fox answered Dan. "She was drunk and happy one moment, then grabbed a knife and tried to stab me."

I shifted back to my normal form. "You won't be able to keep me here forever," I threatened. "I'll escape sooner or later."

Dan arched an eyebrow. "How do you think you'll escape?"

"He's coming for me," I said and smiled. "And he'll kill you for imprisoning me."

"Let him come," Rhys said and growled, his eyes turning into dragon's eyes.

Shifting my hand into a wolf paw with claws extended, I reached through the bars and tried to grab Rhys, but he was just out of my reach. I screamed and swiped my clawed hands at him.

They always stayed just out of my reach.

The five males left the room, and I was alone. I screamed angrily and thrashed against the cage. I sat and began blowing fire on the ceiling of the cage. And all metal melted if heated to a high enough temperature.

Covering myself in dragon's scales, I jumped up out of the hole in the cage. Then, I leapt straight up through the house, through three floors until I made it out into the open air.

"Jolie!" Dan yelled from inside the house.

I was finally out of Nico's range, so I teleported to the park and immediately shifted into my combined form. The princes would come and when they did, I would destroy them.

As expected, the four males found me quickly. They stood in a line before me, scowling.

"Just let me go," I said angrily.

"Go where?" Rhys asked.

"Home," I said.

"Your home is with us," Fox said softly. "We are your mates."

"You tricked me," I snapped. "All of this is a lie."

"I'm going to tear his head off," Deryn snarled.

"Why do you think that?" Nico asked me.

"Brayden freed me from your spell," I explained. "He showed me what you've been doing to me."

"He's the one manipulating you," Fox said calmly. "You can feel us through our bonds. You can sense our feelings. We love you."

"I don't feel anything now, thanks to Brayden," I snarled. "You can't toy with me anymore."

"Yep, I'm going to kill him," Deryn muttered.

"You have our bloodstones," Fox whispered. "You can't fuse them unless it's voluntary. We did not force you."

I reached up with clawed fingers. "I'll remove them."

Nico held out his hand and metal cables wrapped around my arms, pinning them so I couldn't reach my face. When had he learned to do that?

I screamed in pain and Deryn punched Nico's shoulder.

"Ow," Nico said.

"You're hurting her," Deryn growled at him.

"Would you rather she clawed the bloodstones out of her face?" Nico asked.

Deryn growled in response.

"I didn't think so," Nico grumbled and rubbed the spot Deryn had punched.

I shifted into a dragon, my scales protected my bones as I did, and the metal cables fell away. I roared and spit flames at them.

Rhys shifted and roared back, making me cower and take a step back. He was the most dominant male I had ever met. He grabbed the back of my neck with his teeth and bit down, hard enough to hurt, but not hard enough to draw blood.

I was supposed to submit. Part of me wanted to submit. But, Brayden had shown me how manipulative they had been. I couldn't stay here. I had to leave.

Dropping down slowly, he believed I was submitting, but as I neared the ground, I leapt up and clawed his eye nearest me.

He roared in pain and stumbled back two steps.

I shifted into my combined form as the other three approached and fought them in earnest. None of them had drawn weapons, but Deryn and Rhys took warrior forms to better protect themselves.

Nico used a spell to freeze me, but I teleported across the park and out of his range.

"Who taught her to teleport?" Nico snarled.

I couldn't just run. No. I had to defeat them. I had to rid the world of their manipulation so no other girls fell for their ploys.

In my combined form, I charged Deryn, cutting his shoulder and kicked Rhys in the chest when he tried to grab me.

If Brayden hadn't blocked their bonds, I would feel their pain. I was glad he had thought to block them.

Where was Brayden? He had said he would come for me.

Fox tried to use plant vines to tie me up, but I burned them before they could touch me, then used my powers to tie his legs with vines. He cursed angrily and tore at them.

Rhys tackled me from the side and pinned my hands above my head while he sat on me. "Stop trying to hurt us."

"You must die!" I screamed.

"He's controlling you!" Rhys yelled. "Don't you see that? He is controlling your mind and you are letting him."

Drawing in a big breath, I exhaled fire, but Rhys just laughed.

"Your fire doesn't hurt me, Sunshine."

I shifted into my warrior wolf form and rolled us over, so I was atop him now.

Deryn wrapped his arm around my throat and squeezed, cutting off my air. "Don't fight me. Just go to sleep. Please."

I clawed deep gouges into his arms, digging in until I scraped bone.

He growled, but held on, his arm tightening even more.

I collapsed in his arms and held my breath.

"Fuck!" he yelled and pushed me onto my back on the ground.

"Deryn!" Nico snapped.

"She's not dead," Deryn said. "I didn't kill her."

My eyes snapped open and I exhaled fire. He jumped back, yelling in pain. Fox ran to him, using his healing magic to treat the burns.

I stood and faced Nico. His anger was palpable.

"I'm done. You're not yourself," he said. His body began to glow, and I knew I was in trouble.

I opened my mouth and began to sing. All four screamed and clutched their heads. Brayden had taught me a song to hurt whoever heard it. It hurt anyone who wasn't a siren.

The four males clutched their heads as I sang, and blood began to drip from their noses.

Nico lifted his hand and a clear ball formed around me, cutting off all sound. My singing didn't penetrate the ball.

Fuck!

I pounded my fists against the ball, but nothing happened. They were talking and wiping their faces off while staring at me.

My breathing became erratic as I felt the ball closing around me, taking away the air I needed to breathe. I pounded on the ball and screamed, my breaths quickening along with my heartbeat. Fear consumed me, and I tried to shift into a dragon, but the ball was too small. My body reverted, and I screamed. I fell to the ground, gasping for breath.

The ball disappeared, and I gulped in fresh air. That had been too close. I needed to take him out first.

While digging my fingers in the grass, I silently aimed a tree root behind Nico. He squatted down in front of me and I raised my hand. The tree root shot up out of the ground and pierced Nico through his back and out of his chest.

He gasped, and his eyes widened in disbelief as he looked at the root.

"Nico!" Deryn and Rhys yelled.

I turned and ran, headed out of the park, but a force field cut me off, sealing the park off from the rest of the city. Glancing back, I saw Nico with one hand raised, a determined look in his eyes. His other hand pressed around the root and the blood stain spreading outwards from the injury.

I raised my hand, preparing to jerk the root out, but Fox

punched me in the side, making me gasp and drop my hand. I hadn't even seen him.

He pointed his sword at me and snarled. "Stop! Jolie, just fucking stop!"

"Not until you're dead," I whispered.

I tried to teleport but couldn't. I walked slowly up to Fox who watched me but stood still. I snatched his second sword from his hip and pointed it at him.

Tears slid down his cheeks and he whispered, "Please don't do this."

I screamed and swiped at him with the sword.

He easily deflected it. "He's manipulating you, but you're still in there. I know you are. Fight him, Jolie! Fight him!"

I screamed again and attacked, our swords clanging together as he blocked my strikes.

Dammit, they were too strong!

Deryn approached, a sword in his hand. "Baby, you're stronger than him. You can break his hold on you."

I attacked him and yelled, "I only need to break your hold!"

Rhys stood with Nico, his arm around him to keep him standing.

I raised my hand, but Deryn's sword grazed my arm, making me jerk back.

"I am your queen!" I yelled. "Obey me!"

"You can't order us around when you've closed our bonds," Fox said behind me.

I spun and tried to cut him, but he deflected my blade easily.

Out of the corner of my eye, I saw someone new approaching. No, not some one, but multiple people. It was the kings.

"Leave!" Deryn ordered them. "She's not herself."

"That's why we are here," Katar said.

I brought my sword down, aiming for Deryn's shoulder since he was distracted.

Dan caught the blade with his bare hand, blood dripping to

the ground as it cut into his palm. "No," he said and pushed me back. "I won't let you hurt them."

"One is about dead," I said. "I'll finish them off too."

Johann looked over at Nico and his eyes darkened. "Enough playing around." He whispered something and a red circle with magic runes appeared below me. Chains slid up out of the circle and wrapped around my legs and arms.

I tried to pull free, but electricity traveled from the chains into me. I screamed and fell to my knees, my vision swimming.

"Stop it!" Deryn yelled.

"Stop hurting her!" Fox snapped.

"This is the only thing her kind understands," Johann growled.

"And all you understand is defeat at the hands of women," I snarled and began singing, my voice directed at him.

He screamed and clutched at his head, which made the circle and chains disappear.

I shifted into my combined warrior form, well aware that my strength and energy was quickly running out.

Dan and Emrys shifted into their warrior forms and attacked. I kept singing, my voice and powers aimed at Johann, so he couldn't use his magic on me. Fighting the two kings was difficult, but Dan was trying his hardest not to hurt me.

Johann collapsed, so I stopped singing.

"How can you let them do this to me?" I asked. "How can you stand by and let them control me?"

"Brayden is controlling you," Leona said.

I spun around and stared at her in disbelief. "What are you doing here?"

"I came to train you," she said. "If you broke Brayden's hold, you would remember."

She's a traitor. She is trying to steal the throne.

I snarled. "You're after the throne, aren't you?"

195

She rolled her eyes. "You and I both know that I would suck as a ruler. Come on, Jojo. Fight him!"

Jojo? She called me that when were kids.

She wants to keep you chained to the princes.

"I won't be their pawn!" I screamed at her. "I thought we were friends! Why are you helping them?"

Johann tried to put me in a shield, but I held out my hand and made the vine in Nico's chest move, which caused him to scream in pain.

Johann dropped his hands and glared at me. "I should just kill you," he snarled.

"Try it," Nico panted. "I'll destroy you."

Even while I was killing him, he was protecting me from his father?

It's a ploy.

Leona stopped before me and smiled. "Hello, Jojo."

"You're a traitor!" I snapped.

"You're stronger than this," she whispered. "Let me help."

"Help me by killing them," I said.

She began to sing, and pain engulfed my body. I opened my mouth and sang louder than her.

"Barrier!" Dan yelled.

Johann put a barrier around me and Leona, our songs now contained to only hurt each other.

Louder and louder I sang, but Leona was more experienced and with just a different pitch, she broke my concentration and pain engulfed me like being thrown into lava.

I screamed and clutched my head. The princes yelled and tried to come to me, but the kings held them back.

Leona continued to sing, walking closer and closer to me. My legs gave out and I fell to my hands and knees, still screaming.

How could a melody that sounded so sweet cause so much pain?

Kill her!

Brayden. That was his voice. Why wasn't he helping me? Where was he?

"He isn't here," Leona whispered. "He is using a connection he made with you to control you. You can break it and free yourself."

"He's trying to free me from them," I sobbed.

Leona set her hand on my head and whispered, "If that were true, why isn't he here?"

There was logic to her words.

"Let me help you," Leona whispered.

I looked up into my friend's eyes and asked, "Who can I believe?"

She smiled and asked, "Have I ever let you down?"

No. No she hadn't.

She bent down and whispered in my ear, "Fuck you, Douchebag. She's not yours and never will be. Run and hide, because once we find you, you won't survive."

Kill her!

No. I wouldn't kill Leona.

Leona began singing again, her words sliding into my skull and slithering around my brain. It should have felt wrong, but it felt nice. Her powers wrapped around a piece of something in my mind and her voice rose. The louder she sang, the tighter it wrapped, until it snapped the foreign piece and my mind became its own once again.

Free. I was finally free of Brayden.

I LAY ON THE GRASS, LETTING MY BRAIN RE-ACCLIMATE TO WHAT was real, what was truth. Brayden had used his powers on me from far away. He had been able to convince me that my mates were manipulating me and needed to die. I had hurt them. I had almost killed one of my mates!

"Nico!" I screamed, jumped up, and ran towards him.

Johann stepped between us and snarled, "I'm going to kill you."

Nico lifted his hand and knocked his dad out of my way. "Try it and I'll kill you," Nico threatened Johann.

I didn't deserve to be defended by him. I rushed to his side, tears streaming down my face, and reached out to touch his cheeks. "I'm so sorry. I'm so so sorry, Nico. I almost killed you. I was going to kill you. Please tell me you're alright. Please don't die on me."

"He's going to be fine," Katar said and knelt behind Nico. "Kara is on her way and she's going to fix him up."

I turned to Deryn and cringed at his clawed-up arm. "I'm so sorry. I know saying it doesn't help or change anything, but I really am sorry. I can't believe I did all this. I can't believe I hurt you so badly."

Deryn pulled me into his chest with one arm around me and whispered, "You gave us a really big scare. I wasn't sure if we would be able to stop you."

"I'm sorry," I whispered into his chest and sobbed.

"We know," Rhys whispered behind me. "We can feel you again with our bonds."

"How was he able to tamper with our bonds?" I asked, not moving from Deryn's hold.

"He didn't touch the bonds, just blocked them," Johann said with a deep frown.

"Are you okay?" I asked Rhys.

He nodded.

"Fox?"

He nodded too.

"Are you alright?" Leona asked me.

I stepped out of Deryn's embrace to hug Leona. "Thank you. You saved me."

"You saved us all," Nico wheezed.

"Stop talking," I ordered him. His mouth snapped shut and my hands flew to my face. "I'm sorry! I didn't mean to order you. You can talk, just please don't. I don't want you hurting any more than you already are."

"Calm down," Nico whispered and smirked at me. "I'm not dead."

"Jojo, are you alright?" Leona asked again.

I nodded. "I'm fine. You destroyed whatever that was in my head. Now, I'm free of Brayden."

"I really am going to kill him," Deryn said.

"Get in line," Nico grunted.

"Will he be able to do this again?" Dan asked.

I turned and fresh tears appeared in my eyes. I dropped to my knees and bowed to them. "Please forgive me."

"Stop it," Dan ordered me. "You didn't do anything wrong. You were being controlled by that jerk." Dan pulled me up and hugged me.

"You really did save us," Rhys said to Leona. "Thank you."

"You've definitely improved in your fighting," Emrys said and patted my back. "I'm very impressed."

I chuckled and wiped at my tear stained face. "Thanks."

"Alright, who am I healing?" Kara asked as she walked into the park.

"Nico first," Johann said.

Kara patted my cheek as she walked by and knelt in front of Nico. "Did you piss off an elf?" she asked him with a smirk.

"No, just my mate," Nico said and chuckled, then started coughing and wheezing.

"Let's get you patched up," Kara said.

"Will you be able to heal him fully?" I asked her.

She smiled. "Do not worry, Daughter, he will be fully healed and just in need of rest."

"How do we prevent this from happening again?" Johann asked Leona.

"I'm going to teach her how to protect herself," Leona answered.

"Can you teach us how to protect ourselves?" Dan asked. "I don't want that asshole messing with us either."

Leona nodded. "Yes."

"When did you learn those songs?" I asked softly.

"A few years ago. I'll teach you some," Leona promised.

"I don't think her learning new songs is a good idea," Johann grumbled.

"It's better for her to learn all of our songs and abilities," Leona argued.

"I disagree," Johann argued back.

"Good thing you don't get a say," Rhys growled.

"We should all have a say. A siren, especially an empath, is dangerous. Look at what she did today, even untrained. Think about what she will be able to do once she is trained!" Johann yelled.

"Dad, shut the fuck up!" Nico snapped. "It's better if she is trained. Just like it's better for a mage to be trained."

"If you weren't injured, I'd kick your ass," Johann said with a scowl.

"Try me," Nico threatened. "I've been wanting to kick your ass for months."

"Boys," Kara chastised. "I'm not going to heal you just so you can fight each other."

"Your son has had a very bad day," Katar reminded Johann. "Today is not the best day to test his patience."

Johann glared at me once more, then teleported away.

"How did you know to come here?" I asked Dan.

"We felt our sons freaking out and rushed to them, assuming something was happening to you," Emrys said.

"There, all healed," Kara said and stood.

Nico stood up and I took a tentative step towards him. He pulled me into a tight hug and rubbed my back. "I'm fine, Jolie."

I clutched his shirt and sniffled. "I'm sorry."

"Stop," he ordered me.

I obeyed, leaning into him and letting him hold me.

"So, where am I staying? Not that this park isn't beautiful, but I'd prefer to have a house to sleep in," Leona said.

"Let's go get some food," Deryn suggested.

"Come to our house and I'll cook you some food. And, I'll whip up a special potion for Nico," Kara offered.

"Sounds great," I agreed.

Nico offered to teleport us, but Kara refused, stating he needed to rest. So, we waited for drivers to pick us up and take us.

"How did you find us?" I asked Leona.

"You started singing before a barrier was put up. So, I went in the direction the song had come from. It led me here," she explained.

"If we'd known you were coming today, we would have had someone meet you at the station," Deryn said.

Leona shrugged her shoulders. "I like exploring places and don't get enough exercise normally."

"Where is Leona staying?" I asked Nico, whose arms I hadn't left. "I would offer for you to stay with me in my apartment, but I don't have a spare room."

"She is going to stay in Deryn's spare room," Nico explained.

"Speaking of houses," Dan said. "Are you going to stay in those apartments now that you're mated? Or are you going to buy a single house?"

I had been wondering that as well, but kept forgetting to bring it up.

"What do you want to do?" Nico asked me, peering at me sideways.

"It would be nice to have a single house for all of us to be in together," I said. "But, with individual rooms still."

"Where would we buy or build it?" Deryn asked.

"I don't know," I admitted.

"We could buy some land in a neutral area," Fox suggested.

"What about a beach home?" I asked. "I know the sirens own some land not too far from Jinla along the beach."

"We could have several homes," Fox said. "I have one home and—"

"Where would our main home be?" Rhys asked, interrupting Fox.

"Actually," Dan said, getting our attention. "I already bought you guys some property."

"What?" we all asked at the same time.

He rubbed the back of his neck with an awkward smile. "I was going to give it to you as an anniversary present. It's right outside Jinla, in neutral territory."

"How much land?" Deryn asked.

"Fifty acres," Dan answered.

"Fifty!" I gasped. "Why so much?"

"Well, if you do have kids, they're going to need room to run around and play," Dan said.

"And it gives us lots of space to build a karting track!" Deryn yelled.

"Real life karting?" I gasped. "Sign me up!"

"I'll pull up some maps and pictures while we are eating," Dan said with a happy smile.

I hugged him and kissed his cheek. "You're the best father-in-law ever."

"I heard that!" Katar and Emrys yelled.

I chuckled and the guys laughed too.

"What would you like to eat?" Kara asked.

"Fudge!" I yelled.

Everyone laughed.

"You can't eat fudge for a meal," Fox scolded me.

"Why not?" I pouted.

"How about I make a surprise meal?" Kara offered.

"That would be best," Rhys said.

Our drivers arrived and we all traveled to the elf's territory where Kara cooked a huge banquet. Everyone ate and laughed and spent time together.

We had to find our enemies soon and kill them. But, at least we had each other. Leona fit in perfectly and it was like she had always been part of our group. She teased the guys more than I did, and it was nice to have another girl around.

Life was hard, but with friends at my side, I knew I could get through any situation.

EPILOGUE

Nico and I stepped into Deryn's apartment to find Leona and Deryn locked in an intense karting battle. I'd introduced Leona to video games and she had become as obsessed as me.

Nico wrapped his arms around me from behind, pulling me back against him. I listened to his steady heartbeat and it relaxed me.

After I'd almost killed him, I had spent a few days attached to his hip. Thankfully, the others hadn't been bothered by it, understanding my need to be with him. I still apologized when I thought about it, but he always reassured me he didn't blame me. I had been under mind control after all.

The game ended with Deryn winning by throwing a shell at Leona right at the finish line. Deryn cheered.

Leona groaned. "I'll get you one day," she promised.

"Time to go," I said, drawing their attention to me.

Leona jogged to me and pulled me from Nico's grip to hug me. "Hey."

I hugged her back and smiled. "Hey."

She punched Nico's shoulder as she walked by him, and out

the door. The guys had been a little worried about another girl living with us, but like me, Leona had grown up surrounded by males and quickly became just another "guy" in the group.

Plus, she was one of my best friends and respected that they were my mates. They would never stray from me, and she would never try to make them. Besides, they weren't the one she had her eye on.

Once outside the building, we all smiled at Thor who waited by the SUV for us. Instead of returning to his previous job, he'd opted to stay as our driver and bodyguard. Martin had accepted a less dangerous job within the pack, at my urging. Thor said he stayed because he wanted to ensure I was as protected as possible, since both Brayden and Justina were on the loose.

"Hey, Thor," Leona said in a husky tone, her chest puffed up a bit more than normal and her shirt dipped down, exposing more of her cleavage than it already had been.

His eyes dipped for a brief moment, then he met her gaze. "Hello, Leona."

"Just ask her out already," Nico whispered as we climbed into the SUV.

Thor growled softly but made no comment.

We were finally going to see our new house. Rhys and the others had explored the land Dan had purchased for us, and picked out the place our house would be built. Then, Rhys had forbidden us from returning. He drew up the designs and plans for the house and wanted to surprise us all once it was done being built.

"What if it's just a big penis?" Leona asked me.

I snorted. "Maybe if Deryn had drawn it."

Deryn pouted. "Rude."

"Where's Foxfire?" Thor asked.

"He's meeting us there. He had something to take care of with the elves," I answered.

Deryn and Nico sat on either side of me, each of their legs

touching mine. Deryn draped his arm behind me. "Are you nervous?" he asked.

I shook my head. "No, I'm excited. I hate moving but moving into our forever home is worth it. Plus, it will be nice to be in our own house, away from the media."

"Oh, shit! Speaking of media," Thor said. He blindly grabbed for a remote in the center console, then hit a couple buttons. A TV screen flipped down from the roof of the SUV. The screen turned on, showing Dad and Sam standing before a podium with a dozen or so microphones strapped to it, and cameras flashing from the room before them.

"Greetings, I am King Dalton of the Sirens. I come before you today with several declarations. First, yes, it is true that Jolie, Princess of the Four Clans of Jinla, is my daughter and Princess of the Sirens. She has given up her title as heir due to her already heavy responsibilities with the other four clans. She has a set of wonderful mates, and I am very proud of the woman she has become and the things she has, and will, accomplish." He set his hand on Sam's shoulder and smiled. "Sam is our new heir. He is devoted to the Sirens and is one of Jolie's most trusted friends."

The media began yammering, but Dad held up his hand and they quieted.

"Sam and I will be rejoining the Summit next year and apologize for our inactivity the past two decades. We will no longer turn a blind eye to the darkness that is spreading. It is time for all races to work together and bring peace and prosperity to all corners of the world."

"King Dalton," a reporter called out. "Is Jolie still banished from Atlantis and no longer princess?"

Dad smiled, his eyes full of love and joy. "My daughter is no longer banished. She and her mates are welcome to visit us at any time. And, she is, and always will be, our princess."

"He's going to make me cry," I sniffled.

Deryn squeezed my shoulders and Nico patted my leg.

"Why was she banished? Did she break your laws?" another reporter asked.

"Sometimes, we do things as parents, thinking it will be for the best of our kids. Then, we realize we were wrong and must ask for forgiveness. My daughter has forgiven me, and I will do all I can to ensure all Sirens are protected and given the best opportunity to excel in the future."

"That's all the time we have," Sam said, stepping forward. "Thank you."

Thor hit the button and the TV flipped back up. I leaned my head back, looking at the roof of the SUV. It was insane to think about how different my life had been a year ago. So much had happened. So much had changed.

We turned down a road that had recently been paved, but were stopped by Rhys standing in the center of the road.

We climbed out, and he took my hand in his. "Are you ready, my love?" he asked, then kissed my cheek.

I nodded, then we all continued down the road on foot. Foxfire jumped out of the tree line next to us in his fox form. He shifted into his human form, kissed my cheek, and fell into step beside me.

Leona and Thor walked behind us, their arms so close that they no doubt brushed occasionally.

The trees opened and I gaped at the monstrosity before us.

It had four floors, what looked like a helipad on the top, but was most likely a place for dragons to land and take off, two massive wood and iron doors, and over forty windows just on the front. It had wood and rock on the outside, making it look like a cottage. A *giant* cottage.

"It's so big and beautiful," I said, my free hand going to my chest.

"I've heard that a time or two," Rhys said with a smirk.

I smacked his arm, then looked up at him. "It really is magnificent. I love it."

He kissed me and said, "I'm glad you like it. Come on, check out the interior."

"I like it, too," Fox said.

Rhys chuckled. "What about you two?" he asked Deryn and Nico.

"We're reserving our judgment until we see what it's got inside," Deryn replied and Nico nodded in agreement.

The inside was made to look like a cottage as well, with thick, dark wood beams along the ceilings. The first floor had a huge living room, a game room with enough TVs for six people to have their own consoles, and an area with a huge TV for group games, a room with a pool table and foosball table was beside that room, and then a theater with reclining leather seats and projector. There were also a few guest bedrooms.

The second floor had all guest bedrooms. The third floor held rooms for each of us, including Leona and two extras, and a room on one side of the house made to fit a bed all five of us could sleep in comfortably or even just relax in. The bathroom was enormous, more of a public bath than a bathroom.

"What's on the fourth floor?" I asked while still admiring the bath. He'd even had a spa built in.

Rhys led me upstairs, pushed open a set of double doors, and I gaped.

A huge ballroom took up the entire fourth floor.

"Why not have this on the first floor?" Leona asked. "People are going to walk through your personal areas to get here."

He shook his head and pointed at the other end of the room where another set of double doors stood. "That is an elevator from the rear of the house. People will come down a different road than you used, which will deposit them to that elevator."

"You thought of everything," I whispered and pulled him down with a hand on the back of his head to kiss him.

"You forgot the one thing I requested," Nico objected.

Rhys pulled away from me and smiled at his friend. "That area is underground. I figured that it was safer to have it there."

"What?" I asked.

"Nico's lab," Rhys replied.

Nico took off in search of his new playground.

"I'm going to check out my room," Leona said. "Thor, can you come help me rearrange some of my furniture?"

"Sure," he said.

I gave her a knowing smile and she winked at me before trotting off with Thor on her heels.

"Mira," Rhys said loudly.

"Yes, Prince?" a disembodied voice replied.

"Ballroom music, please," he requested.

"Acknowledged," the voice said.

Music began playing, and Rhys swept me into a dance around the room.

"You made it a smart house?" I asked.

He nodded, continuing to lead me in a dance I remembered learning from my father as a young girl. Having my memories back was great, because I remembered all of my ballroom lessons.

"She's programmed to do lots of things. Try it out," he offered.

"Mira?" I called.

"Yes, Princess?" she replied.

"Play my favorite song," I ordered, a smirk on my face, thinking I had thought of something he wouldn't have programmed into her.

"Acknowledged," she replied.

My favorite song began playing.

I halted our dance and blinked back tears.

Rhys caressed my cheek and whispered, "Welcome home, Sunshine."

MORE FROM CATHERINE BANKS

Song of the Moon (Artemis Lupine, Book One)
Kiss of a Star (Artemis Lupine, Book Two)
Healed by Fire (Artemis Lupine, Book Three)
Taming Darkness (Artemis Lupine, Book Four)
ARTEMIS LUPINE THE COMPLETE SERIES (Artemis Lupine,
Books 1-4)
Pirate Princess (Pirate Princess, Book One)
Princess Triumvirate (Pirate Princess, Book Two)
Mercenary (Little Death Bringer, Book One)
Protector (Little Death Bringer, Book Two)
Royally Entangled (Her Royal Harem, Book One)
Royally Exposed (Her Royal Harem, Book Two)
Royally Elected (Her Royal Harem, Book Three)
True Faces (Ciara Steele Novella Series, Book One)
Barbaric Tendencies (Ciara Steele Novella Series, Book Two)
Demonic Contract (Dragon Kissed Trilogy, Book One)
Anja's Secret (Anja of Plisnar, Book One)
Daughter of Lions
Centaur's Prize
Dragon's Blood
The Last Werewolf
Last Ama Princess
Bitten, Beaten, & Loved
Lady Serra and the Draconian
Alys of Asgard
Phoenix Possessed
Tiger Tears
Sybil Deceived
Calvin's Alien Adventure

CONNECT WITH CATHERINE BANKS

I really appreciate you reading my book! Here are some ways to connect with me:
www.catherinebanks.com

Follow me on BookBub:
https://www.bookbub.com/authors/catherine-banks

Join my newsletter for deals and snippets:
http://Catbanks.co/newsletter

Like my author Facebook page:
http://www.Facebook.com/CatherineBanksAuthor

Follow me on Twitter:
http://www.Twitter.com/catherineebanks

Follow me on Goodreads:
http://www.Goodreads.com/catherine_banks

www.Turbokitten.us
www.Turbokitten.us/catherine-banks

Purchase items handmade by Catherine:
http://Etsy.com/shop/TurboKittenInd

Printed in Great Britain
by Amazon

38219784R00130